Saddle Tramps

by

Hal Jons

The Golden West Large Print Books
Long Preston, North Yorkshire,
BD23 4ND, England.

British Library Cataloguing in Publication Data.

Jons, Hal
    Saddle tramps.

    A catalogue record of this book is
    available from the British Library

    ISBN   978-1-84262-892-8 pbk

First published in Great Britain in 1963 by
Frederick Muller Ltd.

Copyright © Hal Jons 1963

Cover illustration © Michael Thomas

The moral right of the author has been asserted

Published in Large Print 2014 by arrangement with
Hal Jons, care of Mrs M. Kneller

The Golden West Large Print is an imprint of Library Magna
Books Ltd.

Printed and bound in Great Britain by
T.J. (International) Ltd., Cornwall, PL28 8RW

CHAPTER ONE

'Head 'em out!'

The drover's call carried clear to the high ground where Clint Bellamy idly watched proceedings astride his dun gelding. Two large boulders screened him from the view of the riders below. Experience had taught him to run the rule carefully over any bunch of riders before meeting them in the open. He got out the makings and then paused in the act of lighting his cigarette.

His keen eyes had picked up the spiralling dust made by a couple of riders heading fast to where the drovers worked the hundred odd head of sleek cattle towards the gap between the two humped foothills. Fifty miles north he and his travelling companion, Mex Juarez, had seen the main herd making its leisurely way east, keeping to the South Platte River basin en route for Kansas City or St Louis. Clint had done some mental arithmetic and had concluded that a cloven-footed fortune was on the move.

Down below the drovers became aware of the approaching riders and the boss motioned to two of them to stay while the others raised the beeves' lumbering gait.

Clint's interest rose as the two riders thundered into clear view. One was a girl and her companion was a young tow-headed fellow of about twenty-two. The girl's wide sombrero screened her features from Clint but she sat her foam-flecked roan like a goddess. She held a rawhide whip in her free hand and a pearl-handled gun nestled in a dark leather holster at her side.

'You there!' Her voice came out vibrant and clear, and Clint watched her point with her rawhide whip towards the drovers.

'Just head those steers back where they belong!'

'Reckon they belong to me, Ma'am. Got a bill of sale right here says they're mine.' The trail boss paused as he fished about in his pocket. 'It ain't no fault of mine if that young feller can't hold his liquor 'nough to remember what he does.'

The girl edged her mount forward and peered at a piece of paper the drover held out to her. She glanced a couple of times from the paper to her young companion who sat his horse like a sack, shaking his head from side to side.

'Shouldn't be surprised if he's lost the dinero I paid him,' continued the trail boss. 'He couldn't get back to the card game fast 'nough.'

There was a long minute when nobody moved. The trail boss sat his mount calmly, his two helpers, one each side, hunched in the saddle both watchful. The girl had let her riding whip fall to her side and the youngster's hand was close to his six-gun.

Clint eased his Colt into his hand just in case he needed to take sides, then reholstered it as the girl came to life. She swung the sweating roan round and without a glance at her companion rode away as rapidly as she had come. The youngster made as if to speak then thought better of it and turning his horse, followed the girl at a slower speed. The trail boss let out a deep belly laugh that was echoed by his henchmen as the three of them set off towards the gap in the wake of the fast moving cattle.

It was then that Clint lit his cigarette and watched the dust spurt as the girl widened the gap between her and the young puncher. He smoked the cigarette to the end, stubbing it out on one of the boulders beside him, then with a shrug of his wide shoulders, he jogged the reins and guided his gelding into the open, down on to the Dallin trail.

A couple of hours later he recounted the incident to Mex Juarez as they sat in the Straight Flush saloon over a couple of glasses of bourbon.

'Looks like the girl and young feller are brother and sister,' said Mex with a grin at Clint. 'And to my way of thinking the young feller's selling stock over her head.' He took

7

a sip of bourbon and waited for it to course its way through his tubes. 'Better him than me,' he added. 'Ain't nothing worse than a sister for cutting a man down to size.'

Clint nodded. 'I guess she was riled plenty. Looked as though she had plenty sand too. How's that paint of yours?' he asked, changing the subject.

'I guess his leg's good enough to move on tomorrow, but I'd like it better if he rested up a couple more days.' Mex smiled quietly as he noted the satisfaction spread over his young companion's face. The girl must have made quite an impression on him.

'Waal, we've got all the time we want,' replied Clint. 'Can't say that Dallin's the best town we've hit but it'll do.'

They drank up and wandered out on to the sidewalk. They leaned over the rail and watched Dallin go about its business. There wasn't much to watch. A grizzled rancher was haranguing the storekeeper outside the ironmongers while his pair of raw-boned greys flicked their tails incessantly at the flies and shifted their weight from one side to the other. Now and again one of them slewed its head around as if to squint at the load of wire and nails in the open wagon. Its expression held no enthusiasm.

A buxom middle-aged woman in black bombazine framed the store doorway checking on the colour by daylight of a bolt of bright material. The stage outside the depot looked permanently at rest, a thick coating of alkali making it appear unreal. Along the sidewalk in the shade a number of oldsters and cowhands lay with sombreros over their faces, sleeping out the last minutes of their siesta.

Mex searched in his shirt pocket and extracted one of his evil-looking cheroots. He chewed at the end and savoured it awhile before lighting up.

'Mighty peaceful, Clint,' he remarked. 'Too peaceful. I've got a notion that Dallin's waiting for something almighty big to happen.' He drew the rank smoke deep into his lungs with keen enjoyment and sent the fumes spiralling as he exhaled. Clint Bellamy shuddered. He eyed Mex with respect on his weatherbeaten homely face.

'Reckon your lungs must be as tough as a maverick's hide to stand up to that punishment,' he growled, moving away slightly out of range. 'You sure you ain't smoking the wrapper?'

Mex laughed, showing white even teeth. 'Can't see what you're bellyaching about. These cheroots are mild enough for a school ma'am. Wait until we get to El Paso. I'll get me stocked up with my favourites – Pedro's – then mebbe you'll have something to holler over.'

Clint groaned and reached for the makings

in self-defence. He looked up and down the main street then back to Mex, and although the street was like an oven, he shivered momentarily.

'I guess you've got an instinct for trouble, Mex,' he said soberly. 'Mebbe what Dallin's waiting for ain't far off.'

Mex didn't reply and they stayed where they were until the loungers and oldsters fidgeted at the end of their sleep, then they turned their steps towards McGraw's Hotel intent upon a sluice down and a feed.

Dallin livened up considerably after sundown. Shafts of light from the saloons split the gloom throughout the length of Main Street and the noise stepped up with each passing minute.

Clint and Mex turned into the Straight Flush saloon and took up a table near one where a card game was already in progress. Clint recognised one of the players as the youngster he had seen earlier in the day with the girl. The youngster had his back to them but there was a tenseness about the way he sat that implied the game meant a lot to him. Clint leaned over to pour out a couple of glasses of bourbon from a bottle the barkeep had just brought to the table and muttered the information to Mex, who glanced at the youngster then at the other players.

'Reckon that young hombre's gonna be short some more stock by the time the night's done,' he remarked quietly. It looked that way to Clint also. The chips were piled up front of the players sitting opposite the youngster. One was a debonair keen-eyed professional gambler dressed in a black Prince Albert, coloured waistcoat and string tie, the other a solemn-faced puncher who kept sneaking glances at a tall, well-dressed rancher standing some way behind the young player.

The two pardners smoked and drank sparingly and as the minutes sped by the build up of tension at the card table spread around the saloon. Eventually both Clint and Mex had their attention riveted on the players and a crowd had gathered around the tall rancher.

The gambler took a speculative look at his cards then placed them face down on the table. His pile of chips had diminished considerably.

'Guess that lets me out,' he remarked with a philosophic shrug of his thin shoulders.

The puncher darted a quick glance at the tall rancher and pushed the rest of his chips into the middle.

'Y'know, Mal,' he said easily. 'I don't reckon you've got the dinero to cover what's down, leave alone raisin' enough to call me.'

Mal stiffened in his chair. He palmed his cards and turned his head around. The tall rancher stepped forward.

11

'You offered me a price for the Rafter K, Steve,' Mal said. 'That price still going?'

'Yeah – the price still goes. But I sure hate to see you stake it on a call.'

'You satisfied Colville?' the youngster snarled at the puncher.

Colville nodded. 'When Steve Mitchell says the money's there, I ain't worried none,' he replied. 'What're you doing?'

Before Mal could answer the batwing doors swung wide with a crash and the girl Clint remembered stormed a furious passage past tables and spectators towards the card players. She was followed by an apologetic looking lawman.

Clint followed her progress admiringly. Her temper did nothing to mar her beauty. A mass of wavy black hair surrounded her oval face and her dark blue eyes flashed fire beneath nicely arched eyebrows. She wore a plain white blouse above a deep brown divided skirt and shiny tan knee-length riding boots.

The card players eyed each other as she pushed her way through to the table and the youngster gaped at her in astonishment and alarm. Steve Mitchell moved forward to restrain her then thought better of it.

With a flourish she leaned over the players and swept chips and cards on to the floor then without hesitation she slammed the youngster across the face hard.

'The game's over,' she gritted. 'And you'll play no more Mal Barrett. You're not gambling away my share of the Rafter K and there's no more of your share left.'

Mal Barrett gazed stupidly at his sister and a hush settled over the Straight Flush saloon. The girl's pearl-handled gun was in her hand and she looked mad enough to use it.

'I guess you're too late to alter things, Miss Stella,' the solemn-faced puncher said. 'Seems the Rafter K hangs on his next call.'

Mal Barrett flashed a quick look at the puncher who had one hand under the table and an expression as furious as his sister's convulsed his features.

'If Mal calls, I'll put a bullet through you Colville,' Stella Barrett snarled then she stepped back as Mal thrust his chair away and stood up.

'You cheating coyote, Colville!' yelled the youngster. 'And you, Faro! You just palmed him a card.'

The puncher put his hands flat on the table.

'You've been drinkin' a mite too much Mal. If you was cold sober I'd take you up on that.'

'You're a pair of thievin' four flushers and I'm gonna get every red cent back that you took me for.'

The gambler, Faro, made a surreptitious move inside his coat with one hand, and

Mal Barrett went into action. Foolish and irresponsible he might have been, easily duped and impressionable but one thing was for sure, he was way ahead of most at gunslinging. Faro died with his hand still an inch or so away from his shoulder holster. There was shock on Colville's face but he stayed immobile as Faro slumped forward.

'He went for his gun,' Mal Barrett said simply. He half turned to Steve Mitchell. 'You saw the way of it, Steve?'

The big rancher shook his head, a look of sorrow on his face.

'Reckon you were in the line of vision Mal. I didn't see anything.'

Stella Barrett stood staring at Faro's body and the gathering pool of blood in stupefied silence. She only came to life when the Marshall stepped alongside Mitchell. Both Clint and Mex had seen the passing of a card and the gambler's move for his gun but wisely they held their counsel. There was more going on in the Straight Flush saloon then appeared on the surface.

'Any of you fellers see Faro go for his iron?' the Marshal enquired of the ring of men. No one spoke.

'Anyone see any card faking?' Again no one spoke.

'Waal, looks like you earned yourself a necktie party, Barrett,' the Marshal continued. 'I'm sorry, Miss Stella,' he added as

14

the girl gasped.

Mal Barrett swung around so that he had his back to the bar. His guns swept around the saloon in menacing arcs. There was a look in his eye that said he had grown up in the last couple of minutes.

'So that's it, eh?' There was a tight smile on his face as he glared at the occupants of the crowded saloon. 'Think you've got me nicely sewed up. Waal you ain't! I'm gonna get back from you leeches every durned thing you've cheated me out of, and if you force me to go wild, the lead's gonna fly. Now – just make a path for me. I'm headin' out. Anyone getting itchy fingers will die as sure as hell.'

'I guess I saw that tinhorn reach for his gun.' Clint spoke up loudly, ignoring the warning look Mex flashed at him. Everyone turned to look at him and Mal Barrett nodded his thanks.

'You keep outa this,' the Marshal snarled at Clint. 'I saw all I wanted for myself. Barrett might get outa town now but he ain't gonna get outa paying for his promiscuous lead-slinging.'

'I'll be testifying to what I saw,' replied Clint.

'Me too,' put in Mex.

'We ain't interested in what a couple of saddle-bums say they saw,' the Marshal said nastily.

'Stow the talking,' said Barrett icily as he

15

moved forward from the bar. The crowd fell away and the youngster prodded the Marshal in front of him. 'Try and stop me, and Leverson gets a slug in the back,' he announced.

Nobody moved as the Marshal preceded Barrett to the door. At the door the youngster holstered one gun and palmed the lawman's guns to the floor. Then he pushed Leverson to one side and dashed out into the night.

There was a marked reluctance on the part of Marshal Leverson to present himself as a target at the door. He dusted himself down and stalked back towards the bar. Everyone was talking now and Steve Mitchell had a protective arm across Stella Barrett's shoulders. Leverson stopped at the two pardners' table. His bulbous face worked as he glared down at them and his dangling moustaches waggled as he spat out his words.

'I don't want to see you saddle-bums around come sun-up.'

Clint stood up and the good humour faded from his face. His square stocky figure held plenty of menace.

'You find a good reason for that Marshal and we'll play it your way but if it's just a matter of your preference you're gonna be plumb unlucky. You push your luck too far and mebbe you won't see sun-up.'

'Let it go Leverson,' bawled out the rancher Steve Mitchell. 'One dead man's enough.'

The Marshal dragged his eyes away from

16

Clint and nodded slowly. 'Yeah – I guess so. Reckon I'll take you up another night if you're around,' he muttered as he pushed on up to the bar. Clint sat back down and Mex poured him another glass of bourbon.

Stella Barrett slid out from under Steve Mitchell's arm and turned to look at Colville. The cowboy had stood up and moved away from Faro's body.

'If Mal said you were cheating Colville, it's my guess you were,' the girl said in a clear voice. 'And I reckon every game he's played has been crooked. The Rafter K will not honour any debts incurred through crooked card games.'

Colville spread his hands and shrugged his resentment away.

'You're all het up Miss Stella,' he replied evenly. 'It's my guess you panicked that brother of yours by storming in and the only way he could get out of making the call that would have put the Rafter K in the pot was by making a ruckus. He sure enough did that.'

'There's nobody gonna press you to pay up on gambling debts, Stella,' Steve Mitchell boomed. 'But I've knowed Colville and Faro a long time and you can take my sayso that they played it straight.'

There was a general hubbub of assent from the knot of men near to Mitchell and Stella Barrett bit her lips in consternation as all the implications crowded in upon her.

The batwing doors swung open again and in walked the trail boss who had driven away the Rafter K cattle earlier in the day. He was followed by a couple of tough-looking drovers. Nobody took much notice of them as they made their way to the bar. They ordered drinks and turned to ask the nearest man what had happened.

Clint leaned over and told Mex where he had seen the trail boss before but his attention was still riveted upon the group of men at the bar. He caught a brief gleam of recognition between the trail boss and Steve Mitchell.

'Waal, I guess Barrett's gotta be brought in,' said Marshal Leverson in a voice that drowned all other noise. 'I'll want a dozen men to ride with me.'

There was a general clamour as men surged forward to offer their services. Stella Barrett watched them with a set face. The trail boss stepped away from the bar and pushed his way to the front. He tapped the Marshal on the shoulder, making the lawman swing around.

'Mebbe I'm talking out of turn Marshal,' he said in a drawling voice. 'But there ain't no profit in chasing some trigger-happy coyote in his own run. Could be a lot of fellers'll get to Boot Hill a bit earlier than they'd like.'

Leverson flashed a quick look at the trail boss.

'Could be,' he answered. 'And what do you think should be done?'

'Waal – mebbe you don't know it but Wilt Shand is in Sterling. Saw him there a couple of days ago. If I was in your place, I'd stick a price on that killer's head and call in Wilt Shand.'

The name of Wilt Shand had an immediate effect on everyone and there was a general shout of approval. Stella Barrett looked at Mitchell in horror and he managed an expression of concern.

'We all known Shand's reputation,' put in Mitchell. 'I ain't so sure that we want him.' Another quick look passed between him and the trail boss who turned again to his drink.

'I guess you fellers know best,' he said. 'Mebbe you like swapping lead up in the hills. Now me – I'd leave it to Shand.' He said it in loud enough tones for everyone to hear but in a completely disinterested manner and it was taken up by the others with loud shouts of agreement. Mitchell's half-hearted opposition was swept aside.

Marshal Leverson called a nearby puncher. 'Hey – Windy! You can ride to fetch Shand. Go and get saddled up and I'll write out a message for him.'

'Sure thing Luke. I'll have my warbag packed muy pronto.' The puncher elbowed his way out and Stella Barrett followed rapidly in his wake. Although visibly shaken by the turn of events, her head was held high. Steve Mitchell spoke a few quiet words to Leverson and hurried after her.

'Y'know, Mex,' said Clint quietly. 'It's my guess that girl and her brother are gonna need plenty of help – and soon.'

'Anyone with Shand on his tail will need luck and a lot of help,' replied Mex. He drank his drink quickly and stood up. His eyes gleamed as he considered Clint's concern. 'Mighty nice looking gal that Stella Barrett. Can't say I'd mind having her for a boss. Let's go and see if she's taking on hands.'

When they got outside they heard the tail-end of the conversation between the girl and Steve Mitchell.

'No Steve – I'd prefer to ride by myself,' she was saying. 'I've got a lot to think about. I'll be alright.'

'Well, if you say so Stella,' Mitchell replied. 'You can count on me for any help you want. And don't forget if you want to sell out, I'll give you top price.' He paused. 'And you know Stella, if you don't want to leave this range, there's a place for you at the Lone Star.'

'Thank you, Steve,' she said quietly. 'You've been kind to me.'

She hauled her mount away from the hitch-rail and rode into the night. Steve Mitchell stayed in deep thought for a moment then turned abruptly, bumping into Mex. He elbowed his way past and re-entered the Straight Flush saloon while the two pards made their way to the livery stable.

CHAPTER TWO

Clint and Mex had been riding an hour or so before they caught up with Stella Barrett. Mex had decided to leave his pinto at the livery stable and had taken his time over selecting his borrowed mount so the girl had got off to a good lead.

They rounded a bend in the trail that ran beside the sheer walls of Three Buttes and hauled their cayuses to a slithering stop a few yards from the pearl-handled revolver that covered them. The moon was high and full and spread a ghostly sheen over the girl's face. She sat her horse as still as a statue, calm and resolute.

'Just stay there,' she said in clipped tones. 'Don't make any quick moves or one of you will die – maybe both of you.'

'Now take it easy, Ma'am,' said Clint coolly, 'don't get jumping to conclusions. We sure don't mean any harm to you.'

'Who are you? And where are you heading?' she asked.

'Name's Bellamy – Clint Bellamy and my pardner's handle is Juarez, Mex for short.' Clint paused. 'And if you're heading for the Rafter K then that's where we're heading.'

Stella eased her mount forward a little and peered at them but without relaxing her aim.

'You're the two men who spoke up for Mal back in the Straight Flush, that right?'

Clint nodded and Mex said 'Yeah.'

'And what do you want at the Rafter K?' she asked in a flat voice.

'Waal, it looks to us like you need a couple of tight hands,' drawled Mex. 'And we got time to spare afore we push on outa the territory.'

'I'm not taking on hands,' Stella Barrett replied. 'For the simple reason there are no beeves left to punch.'

'Now look Ma'am,' Clint said earnestly. 'I reckon we can see the way of things. That's why we spoke up back in Dallin. We don't aim to see a woman pushed around and we'd like it fine if you'd take us on the payroll. That is, we can get along without pay as long as we're free to use the bunkhouse. But if you think your own hands can handle what looks to me like big trouble without us, we'll head back for Dallin.'

'Hands!' She echoed the word in a hollow way. 'I'm left with a crew of one and he's got one arm.' The pearl-handled gun disappeared into its holster and she relaxed herself in the saddle. 'I guess I'll get by,' she continued. 'I've got friends I can turn to. There's no need for you two to take up my troubles especially when I can't pay for your hire.'

'Have it your way Ma'am,' put in Mex blandly. 'So we ain't gonna work for the Rafter K. But we'd be a mite obliged if you could stretch your hospitality to let us use your bunkhouse for a while. Dallin is sure enough pizen to me and my pard.'

Stella Barrett shrugged her shoulders and turned her mount around.

'You're welcome,' she said. 'But don't step out of line. If I find you're not on the level you'll have Steve Mitchell to deal with.'

Clint and Mex glanced at each other and grinned. The trail was wide and they rode on each side of the girl. For a long time they rode in silence but Mex, with his easy suave manner, eventually got underneath Stella Barrett's reserve and by the time the ranch buildings came into view they knew enough of her problems. She told her story quite simply without a trace of self-pity.

It appeared that her parents had been killed three years earlier by a band of marauding Indians led by Chief Crooked Tooth who had broken out of the Nation. Stella had been at school back East and Mal had been in Dallin with the Rafter K hands watching a rough-riding circus. Mal had never recovered from the shock of finding the mutilated bodies of his parents and had taken to drinking more than was good for himself. The few hands with some sense of loyalty had hung on for as long as possible but in the end Mal's improvident drinking and gambling had driven them away. He had gambled away all of the money that Doug Barrett had amassed and the last hundred head of cattle had been sold to a trail herder the previous night in the Straight Flush saloon to keep the card game going. The only stock left was what had disappeared into the thick brush country bordering the north mountain section, and a dozen mustangs that Mal had broken himself.

'I guess I've waited too long for Mal to pull himself together,' she said at length as they rode past a long corral. 'I'd have done best to take up the offers I've had for the Rafter K then Mal couldn't have got himself into the trouble he's in now.'

'That's as mebbe,' said Mex. 'Looks to me like that brother of your'n has been helped into trouble. And to my way of thinking it's trouble that can be solved.'

Stella didn't answer. She had seen the two horses hitched outside the ranch-house, one with a well-filled Aperejos saddle. As she gigged her mount into a faster gait, the ranch-house door opened and her brother appeared, six-guns in hand. He was followed by a stocky-looking oldster with one arm.

'Mal!' Stella called as she hauled her horse to a stop. 'Where are you going?'

Clint and Mex eased their horses and stopped a dozen or more yards away.

'Who are those two hombres?' grated Mal Barrett, ignoring the girl's question.

'They're friends,' Stella answered.

'Friends!' Mal snarled. 'I reckon a man's got only one friend and that's his gun. You fellers can hightail it back to where you came from. I want no so-called friends balling up my pitch from now.'

'Mal! That's no way to talk,' said Stella, coming alongside him. 'These men have already given intention to testify in your favour after tonight's affair.'

'Yeah. I remember. Reckon I'm grateful to you,' Mal said but he kept the six-guns pointing unwaveringly at the two pardners. 'But nobody's gonna testify for me 'cause no one's taking me in,' he continued. 'Mal Barrett's just woken up to himself.' He whispered a couple of words to his sister then stepped down from the verandah.

'Just one thing, Barrett,' put in Clint. 'Did you sell those beeves to that trail boss like he said.'

Barrett looked up at Clint sharply. 'What do you know of that?'

'I saw the beeves being headed out and

heard what the trail boss had to say.'

Mal Barrett shook his head.

'Nope. I sold him none but there was no point in saying so. I guess it was easy to get my signature in Dallin. I'd signed enough notes on account of shady card dealing.' There was a trace of bitterness in his voice. 'It was no time to take up the quarrel with Sis breathing down my neck. She might have got hurt. But I'm taking it up right now, and I'm backing my sayso with lead.'

'Leave things as they are, Mal,' Stella said anxiously. 'They're putting a price on your head and sending to Sterling for Wilt Shand the bounty hunter. Get away into Mexico and stay away until the trouble's blown over.'

Mal turned around slowly to face his sister. There was an air of resolution about him and he had acquired a new dignity in the last few hours.

'I'm not leaving Rafter K territory for any bounty hunter. Shand can take his chance. I'm going under cover only so as I can hit back at the cheating coyotes who called themselves friends.'

He unhitched the two horses from the verandah rail and after making fast the lead rein, swung himself into the saddle.

'Reckon there ain't nothing you fellers can do 'cept mebbe stick around and see that my sister comes to no harm,' he said to the two pards.

Barrett rode away out of the huddle of buildings and disappeared behind a grove of cottonwoods. Stella hurried inside the ranch-house without a word. Inside she threw herself down on a large settle and cried for the first time in years. The short one-armed man closed the front door behind her and stepped down to the pards.

'My moniker's Hollister,' he said. 'Most folk call me Stumpy. I'll show you where to stable your broncs and where you can stow your warbags then mebbe I'll rustle up a bite to eat.'

'Thanks Stumpy,' replied Clint. 'Reckon you can call me Clint Bellamy and my pard's Mex Juarez. Don't know 'bout you, Mex,' he continued, 'but I'll settle for a mug of cawfee.'

'Me too,' Mex nodded and they followed Hollister who led away Stella Barrett's roan to the stables.

They had seen to the horses and were about to leave the stables when Stumpy Hollister turned and set down the lamp he carried beside an upturned box. He sat down heavily.

'Y'know, this was a mighty fine spread a coupla years ago. Even after that Injun war party killed old Doug and his missus we kept things on an even keel for a time. Mal was mighty shook up and left things to me but the time came when he took over and he

27

started in drinking and gambling. We had to sell stock to pay his debts and that meant cutting down on hands. The drifters went first leaving four of us. Windy Root was found with a hole in his forehead on the edge of the chaparral belt near Peake's Pass. Lloyd Ackers who never quarrelled with anyone was gunned down by Leverson the Marshal who said it was self defence, and Wilmer Brett got himself killed riding one of Mitchell's horses in a rodeo a coupla months back. Seems there's a jinx on the place now.' He paused and taking the makings from his waistcoat pocket, rolled a cigarette with amazing dexterity. He lit it then cast a quizzical glance at the two pards who had taken up squatting positions.

'This trouble that Mal's got himself into might sure 'nough be a blessing. There'll be no more gambling now and with a coupla tight hands I could get the brush country combed for beeves. Might find enough to start a herd going agin.' The oldster let his remarks hang in the air while eyeing Clint and Mex from underneath his shaggy eyebrows.

'Waal,' said Mex slowly. 'I dunno whether you Barrett's worth the bother but Clint and me would sure lend a hand for that sister of his.'

Hollister nodded. 'Glad to hear you say it. Now mebbe young Mal don't seem much to you being strangers but he's got mighty good stuff in him that's gotta show agin purty soon. He was a fine young feller till the Injuns killed his folk.'

'You know Wilt Shand will be tailing him pretty soon,' said Clint.

'Yeah, I heard you say. But I ain't worried so long as Mal keeps off the liquor. Shand'll have to be a shade better'n his reputation if he's gonna outgun Mal.'

'Men like Shand don't fight face to face,' Mex put in. 'From what I've heard he's a mighty fine tracker and always gets the edge on the man he's after.'

Hollister stood up and made for the door.

'You pick yourselves out a bunk and I'll get some cawfee along to you,' he said. 'I reckon some shut-eye'll do us more good just now than all the palavering.'

Clint and Mex followed in his wake and after a couple of steaming mugs of coffee settled down in the bunkhouse for what was left of the night.

They had breakfast just after sun-up, cooked by Hollister who seemed to manage things as well as any other man with two arms.

He kept darting quick looks at the pardners as they stowed away a couple of prime beef cuts and large helpings of nicely browned onions and his expression became more and more satisfied each time. He paused in the act of pouring out a couple of mugs of coffee.

'There's just one thing I oughta tell you fellers if you're set on working for the Rafter K. Your pay'll have to mount up till we get 'nough beef together to make a sale or till we sell a few of Mal's mustangs. In the meantime I've a bit saved up and I'll stand you nights in town till the Rafter K pays its way.'

Clint laughed at the anxious look now covering Hollister's face.

'You just keep cooking like this, old timer,' he said, 'and we'll settle for grubstakes only. That right, Mex?'

'Sure is,' agreed Mex as he pushed his empty plate away and sat back to light up a cheroot. Clint edged away a bit.

'Mebbe you won't find the bargain so good after you've had a noseful of this poison my pard's setting alight,' he said to Hollister with a grin.

Hollister sniffed deeply and his nose wrinkled appreciatively.

'Ain't nothing wrong with that,' he answered. 'Smells like a mighty good tobacco.'

Mex's black eyes gleamed with pleasure and he dug into his pocket for another cheroot. He tossed it across to Hollister who lit it with a stick from the fire.

Clint coughed and grabbing his mug of coffee, stalked out into the clean morning air. At that moment the ranch-house door opened and Stella Barrett came out on to the verandah. Clint returned through the fug of the cookhouse, grabbed another mug, filled it, went back outside and crossed the enclosure to where Stella stood, watching him.

It was only now that she really looked closely into him. In the moonlight of the previous evening he had been just a shadowy figure and in the Straight Flush saloon his had only been another face, but this morning in the bright sunlight, his stocky frame had a reassuring quality and his rugged face transformed into good looks when his generous mouth opened in a smile showing strong even white teeth. She noticed also his crisply curling black hair and thought how thick and strong it was. She blushed a little as her glance fell away.

'I guess you can do with this, Ma'am,' Clint said as he placed the mug of coffee on the verandah rail.

No matter what hell her private thoughts had given her throughout the night, she had weathered them without any adverse effect on her appearance. In fact as Clint looked at her he made a mental note that she was about the nicest looking girl he'd ever seen. He had just got around to thinking how she'd look in a party dress when she took hold of the mug and thanked him.

Their fingers touched briefly and they both became instantly and acutely aware of the other. Clint stammered a little, cleared his throat to say something then stammered some more. Stella found pleasure in his embarrassment and her lips curled in a smile that brought an answering grin from Clint.

Her eyes slid away from Clint suddenly and fastened on something in the distance. Clint slewed his head round and saw the dust puffing up way back on the trail from Dallin.

'Looks like you're gonna have company Ma'am,' he said. 'It's a mite early for visiting – reckon they must have something on their minds.'

Stella didn't answer but her face paled and her eyes grew anxious. Clint drank his coffee down, set his mug on the verandah and turned to await the visitors. Long before the riders drew up in front of the house he had recognised Leverson the Marshal. A couple of the others he had seen in the Straight Flush saloon but he couldn't put names to them.

The riders drew up about ten yards away from the verandah, Leverson in the middle, the others fanned out a little, and cast watchful eyes around the ranch buildings.

Leverson's bloated face had a thick stubble of ginger whiskers and his moustache hung limply over his cruel lips. His eyes were red-rimmed from rye and loss of sleep. He looked sourly at Clint then back at Stella.

'I reckon Mal came here first Miss Stella,' he growled. 'Which way is he headed?'

Clint stole a quick look at the girl who

merely glared at Leverson, her lips set in a grim line.

'You getting brave, Marshal?' Clint asked impudently. 'Thought you had deputised your work to that bounty hunter Shand.'

'You keep outa this,' Leverson snarled. 'And pack your warbags. I don't want to see you around next time I hit the Rafter K.'

'He stays right here,' said Stella. Her voice was quiet and controlled. 'He's on my payroll and I'll say when he goes.'

Leverson laughed. 'Your payroll – that's something. That no account brother of your'n gambled away every last cent the Rafter K could raise.' He paused, shifted his quid of tobacco around his mouth and spat indolently in Clint's direction. 'Now you just tell me which way Mal headed. I want to save Shand some legwork.'

Stella glared at him then turned her back on them and walked quickly indoors. The riders looked at each other and laughed. Leverson slid to the ground and made his way towards the verandah steps. Clint stepped in front of him.

'And where do you think you're going?' he asked.

Leverson's face purpled with rage. He thrust a long powerful arm out intending to sweep Clint out of the way.

'Get outa my way, saddle-bum!' he yelled, then gurgled as Clint slipped inside his outstretched arm and thumped a sharp right to his throat.

Leverson sagged but Clint grabbed his shirt collar and held him up while he pumped a few more vicious blows to the lawman's chin. Out of the corner of his eye he saw Mex and Hollister at the door of the dining-hall so being no longer concerned with keeping Leverson as a barrier between him and the other riders, he let the man drop to the ground like a bale of hay.

Two of the riders were in the act of clawing their guns out of their holsters when a warning shot inched past them from Mex's gun. They froze and Mex and Hollister strolled across closing the gap between them and Clint.

'Reckon you've done sign your death warrant feller,' said one lean hawk-faced rider who had sat stock still the whole time. 'Leverson's gonna be riled plenty when he comes to and he'll be gunning for you for obstructing the law. He ain't gonna be satisfied until he's salivated you.'

Clint cast a cold look at the man who returned the look with interest.

'I'll take my chance,' Clint said simply. 'Just get this carrion aboard his cayuse and beat it. Nobody's going inside this ranch-house without Miss Stella's sayso.'

The hawk-faced man and his nearest companion slid to the ground and without a

34

word manhandled the Marshal on his horse. He was showing signs of recovery but his men didn't wait. They hauled their horses around and headed back towards Dallin, the hawk-faced one leading Leverson's grey.

Clint swung around and looked confused as he saw Stella at the door again. The shot had brought her out.

'I'm afraid all you've done is cause more trouble,' she added. 'But I'm sure your intention was good.' She returned indoors before Clint could say anything so he turned back to Mex and Hollister.

'Waal, looks like things have started to hot up.' Mex's teeth gleamed as he grinned his satisfaction and Hollister had a big smile all over his gnarled face.

'It sure does me good to see that crittur leave the Rafter K with a flea in his ear. Reckon we've eaten humble pie long enough.' He became serious. 'Y'know Clint, you'll sure have to look out for Leverson from now on and Slim Murrow that did all the talking, he'll be all set to get you. Him and Leverson's mighty close.'

Clint simply shrugged his broad shoulders.

'I reckon the time to worry is when trouble comes. Just ain't no use fretting.'

'Yeah, I used to think the same way,' replied Hollister. 'But a while back an awful lot o' trouble came in a rush. It kinda changed my outlook.' His face broke into a grin.

'That ain't saying you ain't right though. Now if you fellers'll clean up the cookhouse while I get some breakfast for Miss Stella, we can get riding all the sooner.'

'I've got a better notion,' put in Mex after drawing deeply on his cheroot. 'You stay and look out for Miss Stella and we'll make a passear through the brush. With trouble coming up there ain't no sense in pushing the critturs into the open where they'll have to be herded. Leave 'em where they are and that leaves us free to look after other things.'

Hollister looked at the Mexican admiringly. 'You sure have got one smart noggin Mex,' he said. 'Yep, I guess that's the sensible thing to do. You might as well get saddled up then.'

Clint and Mex got saddled up and both fitted on the batwing chaps they favoured for brush work. They were just about to ride on their way when they saw another horseman coming in off the Dallin trail. Hollister was just returning from the ranch-house with a tray. He squinted towards the rider and came over to the pardners.

'Ain't nobody to worry about,' he announced. 'That's Steve Mitchell. Reckon he'll be rooting for Mal on account that Mal is Miss Stella's brother. He's all-fired keen on making himself Mal's brother-in-law.'

For some unknown reason this information soured Clint's normal good humour

36

and he swung his mount around with less consideration than usual.

'No sense in staying then,' he growled and kneed the horse into a gallop. Mex's eyes twinkled with laughter as he waved farewell to Hollister and set his horse after Clint at the run.

Hollister set the tray down and scratched his head in perplexity. 'What in heck got into him?' he said aloud then turned back to meet Steve Mitchell.

'Hiya Stumpy! Miss Stella inside?' boomed Mitchell as he hauled his big black gelding to a stop.

'Yeah – just eating her breakfast,' replied Hollister. 'Reckon she'll be pleased to see you,' he added.

Mitchell's handsome face creased into a smile.

'Yep, I reckon she needs her friends just now. Has Mal been here since leaving town?'

'Sure,' nodded Hollister. 'Just to collect his warbag. He didn't stay around long. Anyways you go inside and I'll see to your cayuse.'

Mitchell nodded his thanks, bounded up the verandah steps and after a brief knock at the ranch-house door pushed it open and walked inside. He could tell by Stella's colour as she sat at the table making heavy work of eating that she had heard him arrive and that his presence was bothering her. The fact gave him unlimited pleasure.

'Come right in Steve,' the girl said. 'I'll get Stumpy to fix you up with some breakfast.'

Steve Mitchell thanked her and sitting down, let his eyes follow her trim figure to the door with a look laden with sensual desire. His expression was under control by the time she returned.

'I'm durned sorry that things got outa control last night Stella,' he said as she sat back down. 'I didn't know Mal was getting himself in so deep or I'd have tried prizing him outa that gambling craze of his. When he asked me if my price was still open for the Rafter K, I reckoned he was fooling.'

Stella flashed a look of gratitude towards him. 'You couldn't help what happened Steve. You've done your best with Mal. I suppose he had to come up with something like this to straighten himself out.'

Mitchell allowed his face to assume serious lines.

'I don't want to add to your troubles Stella, but it looks to me like he won't have much time in which to get straight. Faro had a lot of friends in Dallin and the way they're talking, they won't be satisfied unless the score's been evened up.'

'But there were men who said they saw Faro go for his gun,' protested Stella. 'I heard them say they'd testify to that.'

Mitchell shrugged his shoulders.

'Saddle tramps,' he replied. 'That type'll

38

say anything then move on.' He caught the hurt expression in her eyes and hastened to put himself right. 'Mind, I'd be mighty pleased if they stuck to what they said but like I said, they move on. I stayed on in Dallin last night and they hightailed off somewhere. There was no sign of 'em when I pulled out afore sun-up.'

'You're wrong about them Steve,' Stella replied. 'They rode out here with me and they're working for the Rafter K. They've already dealt with Marshal Leverson this morning. I'd have thought you might have met up with Leverson on his way back to Dallin.'

Mitchell looked surprised. 'Nope, I didn't keep to the trail all the way. I reckon I'd better look these hombres over Stella. You're taking a chance with strangers. Could be they're on the run and out to get into your good graces afore helping themselves to what they can find.'

'There's not much left to find, Steve, so I'm not unduly worried.'

'All the same, you want to be careful. What do these hombres call themselves?'

'Bellamy and Juarez,' Stella replied. 'And no matter what you say Steve, while they're prepared to testify that Mal only shot in self defence they are more than welcome on the Rafter K.'

Mitchell didn't press the point but eased

his chair back to allow Hollister to place a meal in front of him. After the oldster had poured out a mug of coffee and departed, the rancher regarded Stella earnestly, allowing a little desire to show in his eyes. Stella felt her colour rising and her heart pumped a little more quickly. She was not too sure of her feelings for Steve Mitchell but his strong frame and handsome features had a way of unsettling her. She knew what he was about to say and she was not so sure that she'd be strong enough to withstand him.

'Look Stella,' he said quietly. 'I feel the best thing for Mal to do would be to leave the territory. You know Shand is on his way to trail him. If he stays around Shand will get him. But if he gets away quickly and keeps going then the price on his head won't be enough to keep Shand trailing.' He paused and took a long pull of coffee while he watched the girl for reaction. Stella merely nodded. 'Now Mal will hang on while the Rafter K is Barrett property. My advice is to sell out and you know I'll pay the top price. The money would give Mal a stake wherever he went and he could lie low long enough for all this to die down. Y'know how I feel about you, Stella?'

His hand reached out and closed over hers sending the blood racing even faster through Stella's veins. 'We could get married so you wouldn't lose the Rafter K after all.'

His grip tightened on her hand as she looked down in embarrassment. His eyes roved over her hungrily and she felt the animal passion of the man vibrate through her.

'I – I'll have to think about it Steve,' she muttered, drawing her hand away. 'It's a big decision to make.' She stood up and paced the room, her brows furrowed through concentration.

'Sure, Stella, think all you want,' said Mitchell soothingly. 'I don't want to panic you into anything you ain't sure about. Y'know I'd give Mal a stake as a handout but that wouldn't make him leave the territory. He'll only go if he ain't got the Rafter K to fight for.'

Stella stopped her pacing and looked at him. The sense of his remarks was obvious and as his handsome features made her catch her breath, she wondered at the reason for her caution. She couldn't honestly say that she loved Steve Mitchell but she didn't doubt that being married to him could be pleasant. She was about to agree when the rugged face of Clint Bellamy flashed through her mind. There seemed to be a warning expression in his eyes.

'If what you decide is gonna help Mal, Stella, you'll have to make up your mind pretty soon.'

'I guess you're right Steve. Thank you for

being so kind and thank you for asking me to marry you. I – I can't think with you here – in fact there's only one way I can think. Will you forgive me if I leave you and go for a ride. If you come back tonight, Steve, perhaps I'll have got myself straight.'

Mitchell stood up and crossed to her. He placed his hands on her shoulders and looked down into her face. His expression was one of concern.

'Yeah, you go right on out and get yourself straight Stella. I'll finish that meal and go back to Dallin. Mebbe I can get the towns-folk to soften up their ideas. Anyways I'll get back tonight.'

'You're very understanding,' the girl replied simply as she headed out through the door.

There was a big grin of satisfaction on Mitchell's face as he sat down to finish his interrupted meal. It looked as though he'd get the Rafter K and Stella Barrett all in one swoop.

CHAPTER THREE

Clint eased up his horse and wiped away the perspiration from his face. Mex pulled up beside him and swinging a leg over his saddle pommel, dropped to the ground.

'Good a place to rest up as any,' he observed.

Clint nodded and dismounted.

The towering heights of the Three Buttes petered out to the foothills that gently sloped down to the trail and the pardners had reached the point where Clint had watched the trail herder take the Rafter K cattle through the gap. Bunch grass was plentiful amidst the red soil beside the trail and a freshwater spring gurgled from out of the hillside.

They watered their horses carefully then ground-hitched them on long reins to graze. After a drink at the spring and a hasty meal out of a couple of cans the two pardners climbed the shoulder of the foothill and viewed the terrain. The molten sun glared down with fierce intensity and once out of the shadow of the foothills the hot wind that swept the wide plain scorched their cheeks. The visibility altered each minute as the haze shimmered and danced.

'Mighty good country this,' said Mex extracting one of his beloved cheroots from his pocket.

'Yeah, sirree,' agreed Clint. 'It's hotter'n all hell but it's sure got something kinda special.'

Mex looked over the top of his cupped hands as he shielded his match from the wind, down at the undulating prairie grass.

'Yep, and if I raised cattle hereabouts I'd go for those short-horn critturs. They carry a whole lot more meat and I guess they'd thrive alright. It ain't likely they'd have to dig for winter graze.'

Clint was about to reply when he thought he detected movement out on the plain. He squinted in the direction but the haze had clamped down again.

'Thought I saw something coming this way,' he said when Mex looked at him questioningly. A minute went by and the haze lifted. This time they both saw the distant huddle of moving animals and the dust spewing up around them.

'They're heading this way,' said Mex. 'And whoever's driving them ain't caring greatly how much meat he's running off 'em.'

The pards flattened themselves down on the hillside and shading their eyes with their hands watched the cattle come clear of the haze and grow in size as the distance diminished.

It was a long time before they were able to pick out cattle from horsemen and when they did they were surprised to find that just one man held the fast-moving bunch together.

'That hombre sure looks like he's playing for big stakes, herding that lot on his lonesome,' remarked Mex, then he laid his hand on Clint's arm as he squinted again with his hyper-sharp eyes. 'That's Mal Barrett, Clint,

44

as sure as you're a splay-toed Texan.'

For a minute or so the rider was around the far flank of the herd and lost to sight, then with the cows running straight towards the gap the rider dropped back a bit, bringing him into clear focus.

'Cripes, you're right Mex. That's the herd the trail boss took on a forged note. Reckon Barrett's got plenty o' gall to get that lot back again.'

'Wonder what he's done to get 'em away from the drovers? He ain't satisfied to have Wilt Shand on his tail, he's gotta stir up war with a bunch of hardened trail waddies as well. I guess I don't blame him but I reckon he's loco to bring the war back to his own stoop.'

The gait of the cattle had lessened considerably and they mulled through the gap below the pards at just above a lumbering walk. Steam rose in clouds from their lathered hides and the sharp smell of them crept up the hillside to where Clint and Mex watched. Mal Barrett rode behind, shiny and black from sweat and trail dust. His clothes hung on him like the limp wet rags they were and his grey mustang only showed its colour in streaks. The animal's flanks heaved from effort and the foam splashed from its mouth at every shake of its head.

Through the gap Barrett came up alongside the left flank of the herd, bunching them against the wall of the foothill.

'Seems he ain't gonna head for the home pasture after all Mex,' said Clint. 'I guess we might as well join up with him. That's the best way to keep on top of what's new.'

They scrambled downhill to where their horses stood and leaping into their saddles, set off after the herd. Barrett saw them while they were still a couple of yards away. He hauled his mustang around to face them and his guns slid into his hands with the speed of quicksilver. Clint and Mex came on warily until just a few yards separated them.

'Right – that's far enough,' snapped Barrett. 'What're you trailing me for?'

'Reckon we just happened across you Barrett,' said Mex quickly. 'Looks like your trail's been mighty hot since last night. You sure have been busy.'

'Busy enough.' The reply was laconic. 'Like I told you, I'm taking back what's mine.'

'Yeah and how many herders did you have to rub out to get them back?' asked Clint.

'Can't see that it's any of your business but the only casualty was one night herder and he's got himself no more than a sore head. It's just possible there'll be some sore feet though afore him and his pards catch up with their broncs.'

'Waal, it looks like you'll need some help to drive them critturs to where you're gonna graze 'em. That cayuse you're forking looks

46

about all in.' Clint reached for the makings as he spoke, ignoring Barrett's six-guns.

Barrett was silent for a full minute while he surveyed the two pardners carefully then he holstered his guns and nodded.

'Yep, I guess you're right,' he said. Clint offered the makings and Barrett eased his mustang alongside to take the tobacco sack and papers.

'I just don't know why but it looks like as though you're both set on helping me. The best way you can do that is by herding these critturs along the line of these foothills to the brush and drive 'em in deep.'

Clint took back the makings and looked to Mex for his opinion. Mex nodded agreement.

'That's where we was headed anyways,' grinned Mex. 'Reckoned to have a count up of Rafter K stock. Just so that your sister knows what's what.'

Barrett didn't answer. He just smoked hungrily until the cigarette was finished. He ground out the stub on his boot and turned his mount to the west. Raising one hand in farewell he rode off at a jogtrot that was just above walking pace. Clint and Mex watched him go until he disappeared over the rim of a small hump.

'There's a lot o' sand in that hombre,' observed Mex. 'I reckon he meant it when he said he was gonna even up all the scores.'

'Yep – the fur's gonna fly on this range. He don't seem worried any 'bout having that bounty hunter Shand on his tail.' Clint stubbed out his cigarette and looked significantly at the steers now bunched and grazing. 'Seems we've gotten ourselves a herd. Let's get the chore done so that we're free to keep tabs on the next moves.'

'You're in an all-fired hurry to get back to the ranch-house Clint. If I didn't know you for a footloose cowboy I'd reckon that you was thinking of settling down.' Mex gigged his horse forward before Clint could frame an indignant reply but he noted when Clint eventually caught up that the Texan was preoccupied as though the remark had set thoughts to work that had only been waiting for a jolt.

They drove the herd easily in the lee of the hills, giving the animals the chance to recoup their strength after their gruelling run. One thing which gave the pardners satisfaction was the fact that the beeves were so tuckered, none of them tried breaking out of line.

It took them about three hours to get to the fringe of the brush and chaparral country, then Clint and Mex put in some solid work driving the animals into the maze of thorny vegetation. They were as reluctant to enter as they would later be reluctant to leave and practically every one had to receive individual attention. The pards were grimed with dust and sweat and bleeding from innumerable cuts by the time the Rafter K cattle were cleared off the range, deep into the brush where they bawled protestingly.

From signs picked up in the course of their work, Clint and Mex gained the impression that the brush held a further hundred and fifty head of cattle – animals that had drifted in and stayed on to multiply and grow wilder with each passing week. They heard a number crashing through the clawing undergrowth away from the scent of horse and man. Both men had the same thought; driving cattle in was alright but there would be plenty of sweat and swearing before they'd be prised out again. Plenty of risk too. All the advantages were on the side of the steer in the brush. To tip the scales a man had to use all his guile, and above all have under him a horse with split-second reactions.

Characteristically they pushed the thought away. Trouble was for when it appeared and emerging once more out of the thickest growth to where wide spaces showed, they rested up and smoked. Mex looked sourly at the horse he had borrowed from the livery stable.

'I guess we'll make the Rafter K in plenty o' time to push on to Dallin,' he said. 'That paint o' mine should be sound enough by now.'

Clint wiped sweat away from his eyes and grinned.

'And what sort of a welcome do you expect in Dallin? That Leverson feller's gonna be hopping mad after that little ruckus this morning.'

Mex's black eyes glistened. 'Waal, if that ain't taught him some sense I guess he deserves what he lets himself in for,' he replied.

They remounted and rode back along the line of the foothills that ran south-east for a few miles. It was their intention to head straight south when the hills veered due east, and by their reckoning they would then hit the Rafter K headquarters in a direct line. When they arrived at the forking point trouble brewed up. Both Clint and Mex saw the huddle of horsemen at the same time and both guessed rightly who they were. They glanced at each other in a resigned sort of way and sat tight to await developments.

When the riders were about a quarter of a mile away Mex unsheathed his Sharps. 'You move on a piece, Clint, and I'll cover you,' he said calmly.

Clint nodded and eased the dun gelding forward to meet the riders. The trail boss was in the lead and his face was dark with fury as he hauled his mount to a stop twenty yards or so away from where Clint waited. The four other men pulled up alongside him. The trail boss looked past Clint to where Mex had his rifle trained on them.

'You're trespassing,' Clint said in a flat voice. 'This is Rafter K territory and from now on no one rides on Rafter K property without the owner's sayso.'

The trail boss's face broke into a sneering grin. 'From what I heard, the Rafter K owner ain't gonna be riding his own territory much long. Wilt Shand'll see to that. Anyways the bustard jumped the night guard last night and drove off the steers he sold me. I aim to get them back.'

'The only steers I've seen belong to the Rafter K,' answered Clint. 'And just to keep things straight, the boss says he never sold you any steers anyways. That kinda makes you a crook as well as a liar.'

The trail boss stared at Clint, stupefied at the young Texan's temerity. The blood of anger suffused his face while his men watched curiously.

'I've got the bill o' sale right here,' the man grunted. 'So it makes no difference what your boss says. You just get outa my way so's I can collect them critturs or you can take what's coming.'

'The palaver's done,' announced Clint. The light of humour faded from his eyes. The trail herders saw him transform from a rugged-looking but feckless youngster into a wide-shouldered menacing destroyer. 'My pard'll send one o' you hombres to Boot

Hill for sure and I'll get the next two. From then the odds'll be even. It's your choice.'

One of the herders was trying to take up a position that would leave Clint between him and Mex's rifle but Clint read the man's mind and kneed his gelding, making the animal edge sideways.

The trail boss cast sidelong glances at his men, trying to gauge the measure of their loyalty and determination. None of them registered any eagerness to do battle but there was no sign that they would back down without some face-saving bluster. He looked back at Clint and shrugged his shoulders.

'You're a regular fire eater, Mister, ain't you,' he said at length with a sneer. 'You'll mebbe get surprised if we all scrabble for our irons. It's likely the odds will work out a mite different.' He drew deeply on his cigarette, letting the smoke curl lazily from his nostrils. 'But we ain't in any hurry to trade lead. Like I told you, we aim to get those steers back and that's what we're gonna do, but we can wait. We'll just mosey along to Dallin and wise up the Marshal 'bout Barrett rustling my steers then the next time we come alooking for 'em you can get yourselves salivated legally.'

Clint didn't bother to answer. He observed a lifting of tension on the part of the drovers. Their boss had thought up a stonewall reason for postponing the battle and with the passing of danger the mockery came back into their faces. The trail boss took up the reins and made to move away, then froze as Clint barked: 'Stay where you are!'

The drover eyed Clint with savage curiosity. 'Waal?' he ground out.

'You can leave your shooting irons with us.' Clint's voice was smooth but definite. 'Just unbuckle your belts and let 'em drop nice and easy. Any one o' you hombres fumble and my pardner'll put a hole through his skull. That right, Mex?' he called out.

'Yep. You're durned right and I ain't got no preferences. Reckon I'll shoot one as ready as another.'

There was a long pause during which time Clint's nerve ends tingled with expectancy. He sat motionless as a statue waiting for the first warlike move. Then he relaxed as the trail boss slowly unbuckled his belt, letting it slip to the ground. The others followed suit and turned their horses to face the way they had come. The boss continued to glare at Clint with malevolent hate.

'If you're smart, Mister, you'll hightail it pronto and leave Barrett to fight his own battles 'cause I'll be back and there's no hombre breathing who's got the drop on Luke Mappin twice.'

For answer Clint went for a gun with smooth liquid speed. Four shots rang out in rapid succession. The first tugged Luke

Mappin's Stetson from his head, the other three went through the Stetson before it reached the ground. Clint slipped down to the ground, collected the Stetson and tossed it to the trail boss. Mappin's colour went a little as he surveyed the neat round holes then, jamming it back on his head, he hauled his horse around and caught up with his men who had moved away a bit before the firing caused them to look around in alarm. They all eyed his headgear solemnly then spurred their horses into action.

Mex brought his mount alongside Clint and placing his Sharps back into its saddle holster watched the drovers go. His normally cheerful face was serious.

'I reckon we're building up a heap o' trouble for ourselves, Clint,' he observed. 'That Mappin's a pretty hard case and when he promises to be back, you can bet your bottom dollar he'll do just that.' He pulled out one of his cheroots and chewed meditatively for a couple of minutes. 'And when he comes back he's gonna bring a strong enough crew to take what he's after. Are you sure that Barrett is worth sticking our necks out for?'

Clint laughed outright, getting an answering grin from Mex.

'Y'know durned well that if I said "No" you'd find a dozen reasons why we've gotta stay just for the heck of it.'

Mex didn't deny the fact and together

they gathered up the drovers' gunbelts.

'Just as well hand these in to that pesky Marshal Leverson,' grinned Mex. 'He'll mebbe take us as law-abiding citizens after all.'

'You sure do like rubbing shoulders with trouble,' said Clint admiringly. 'Once you get inside that gaolhouse o' his, it's gonna take an awful lot to persuade Leverson to let you out.'

Neither of the pards seemed too worried, however, as they remounted and set off towards the Rafter K headquarters. They chatted and smoked in perfect contentment as though removed by a hundred miles from the range war that was brewing.

It was close on sundown when they rode into the Rafter K enclosure. Stumpy Hollister was framed in the cookhouse door and Stella Barrett was pacing the verandah as though the world's problems were on her shoulders. The pards knew she had troubles enough but did not know of course that before the night was out the weightiest of all woman's considerations was hers to solve – whether to accept a man's proposal of marriage or not.

As Clint and Mex stood talking to Hollister, telling him about the latest developments, Stella paused in her restless pacing. Her eyes were drawn to the young Texan's sturdy figure as though by magnetic

55

impulse, and without consciously connecting Clint with her problems she decided at that moment she did not wish to marry Steve Mitchell. Whether for the sake of her brother she would have to go through with it was a different matter. She tried to analyse her feelings and to her surprise was unable to find one reason why she should not marry Steve. He was handsome, strong, considerate and kind, yet forceful in business. A man who would always lead and who would create for his wife a position of respect. But her mind was made up – the reasons would no doubt unfold themselves in due course.

Mechanically she watched Hollister lead the two horses to the stable and her two new hands enter the wash-house. She was still lost in thought a few minutes later when they emerged, shining after a brisk wash. A muscle near her heart gave a quick twist as Clint's berry brown face broke into a beaming smile just before he preceded Mex into the cookhouse, then she knew the reason for her indecision. There was a lot she would have to find out about the footloose cowboy Bellamy before her mind would be free to consider Mitchell's proposal.

The incongruity of the situation made her smile despite her anxiety for her brother. On the one hand was Steve Mitchell, big, dynamic, who had ridden into Dallin six years earlier in company with Colville and

Faro and after starting up in a small way on the Lone Star, had run a trail herd to Missouri, then bought out old Rube Kennett, his big neighbour. Her mind skipped over the troubles that had hit the Kennett spread preceding the sale. There had been troubles enough on the Rafter K. Anyway Mitchell had made his way and was solid enough for any woman to lean on. Bellamy on the other hand, although strongly built, was unassuming to the point where Stella felt he might be ignored. His features taken individually were good but collectively held just an honest homely quality. Only when he smiled did the charm break through. He had sprung from nowhere along with his too handsome, debonair Mexican partner and for all she knew he could stay until he had feathered his own particular nest then move on again. She realised that her summing up could be at fault when she recalled the quiet assurance with which Clint had spoken up on Mal's behalf and the way he had handled Marshal Leverson earlier that day.

Finally she gave up the problem and returned indoors. She was left with a feeling of irritation that Bellamy had sprung from nowhere. If he hadn't arrived there would have been no problem. She could have married Steve Mitchell without quibble and Mal could have cleared out of the territory to safety.

57

CHAPTER FOUR

It was a little later that Clint knocked on the ranch-house door. Stella called out 'Come in' and he entered the long comfortable room diffidently. He was twirling his Stetson as though needing something to fasten his attention upon. Stella stood up and looked towards him questioningly. There was a bewitching quality about her features and Clint stopped the twirling Stetson as his glance fastened upon her.

'I thought you might like to know Mex and me met that brother of yours.'

Stella's hand went up to her throat and she stepped a few paces towards him. Clint raised his hand to reassure her as she framed a question.

'He'd won back those steers the trail herders took on that forged note. That sure took some doing for a man on his lonesome.' Clint paused a moment to admire the look of surprise on her face. 'Mex and me took the herd over and drove 'em into the brush. We can prise 'em out again when things quieten down. Mal pushed on to where he's holing up.'

Stella didn't comment but the worry lines

were etched on her face.

'Your brother didn't get hisself in any deeper,' Clint added hurriedly. 'He just gave the night herder a sore head.'

'Thank you for telling me,' Stella replied. 'I guess I'm glad that you decided to stay around.' She gave him a quick smile and Clint felt the blood pound in his veins as her face lit up.

'Waal, Ma'am, that is, Miss,' he stammered. 'Me and my pard are going in to Dallin. We'll be back well before sun-up.'

'To Dallin?' she echoed. 'Is it safe for you to go there after what happened this morning?'

Clint shrugged his wide shoulders and grinned easily.

'Oh we ain't gonna advertise ourselves any. It's just that Mex wants to collect his own bronc from the livery. The cayuse he's forking makes him kinda sour.'

There was doubt in her eye but she nodded understandingly.

'Waal, I guess I'll be on my way.' Clint inclined his head politely and went out into the night. A short time later Stella heard the two pardners ride away.

Clint and Mex had reached the halfway mark to Dallin when they met up with Steve Mitchell. He looked an impressive sight in the moonlight astride his tall Palomino stallion. He drew rein as he recognised them.

The pardners pulled up to face him.

'Howcome you fellers are lining yourselves up with the Rafter K?' he asked. 'Just what are you after?'

'And what's it to do with you?' Clint replied insolently.

Mitchell leaned forward on the saddle to glare at the Texan. 'The Rafter K is my business,' he growled. 'Anything likely to affect the Barretts concerns me. We've been friends a long time.' He paused to let the information sink in. 'And the way I see it,' he continued. 'When a couple of saddle tramps take sides on a payroll that doesn't exist, they're more than likely playing some crooked game of their own.'

'Yeah. I reckon that's the way you would see it,' put in Mex dryly. 'It's my guess you don't look at anything without weighing up the profit.'

'Anyway,' Clint said, 'I didn't see you so fast to show your friendship the other night in the Straight Flush. A word from you would have put Mal Barrett in the clear. It's my guess you saw Faro go for his gun as clearly as we did.'

Mitchell contained his temper easily.

'My personal feelings have got nothing to do with my duty as a citizen. If I didn't see Faro go for his gun then I'm not going to perjure myself even for a friend. That doesn't mean to say I'm not going to help

Barrett though.' He paused then when neither of the pards said anything: 'That brings me back to you. If you've got some game in your minds concerning the Rafter K, you'd better keep on riding or you'll end up wishing you'd never seen this territory.'

'Ugh – no doubt you're a mighty big man hereabouts, Mitchell,' replied Clint. 'And it's likely you've got enough strings to pull so that things can get mighty hot for us. But so many hombres have told us to hightail out of the territory that my pard and I have become plumb curious to find out what happens if we don't.'

Mex sniggered and lit a cheroot with exaggerated attention, holding the match to the end longer than necessary so that Mitchell couldn't fail to see his sneering grin.

Mitchell shook the reins and gigged his Palomino into action. 'You'll find out soon enough,' he snarled as he swept past them.

Clint and Mex turned in their saddles to watch him as he rode swiftly up the trail until he rounded a bend where a ring of tall cottonwoods screened him from view then they rode on towards Dallin.

'Y'know,' Mex observed with a grin. 'There's one hombre I'd just hate to have for a friend.' Clint just grunted a reply. It was obvious where Mitchell was heading and a pang of jealousy rose up in him as he pictured the tall rancher in cosy comfort with Stella Barrett. Mex was quick to divine the Texan's thoughts and refrained from indulging in light conversation.

When they arrived at the livery stable Dallin was still going strong. There were lights from saloons and dance halls along the length of Main Street and the discordant notes from pianos playing different tunes battled for prominence with the cicadas' unmusical chorus.

They intended to collect Mex's pinto and return immediately to the Rafter K. While the pards never backed down from trouble they had too much good sense to look for it. And with Leverson on the rampage for them Dallin might be a little uncomfortable.

While Mex went inside the livery to trade back his borrowed horse and saddle up his pinto Clint waited outside, leaning easily against the top bar of the corral fence when a horse and rider emerged out of the gloom and swept past him with hardly a sound.

The moon's light was just strong enough for recognition. The rider was Mal Barrett and his horse's hooves were muffled so that it moved like a phantom. Barrett passed out of sight into the darkness until Clint picked the shadowy figure up again as Mal crossed patches of light from the saloons.

Clint pushed his Stetson back and scratched his head in perplexity. What in the name of all things did Barrett think he was doing? Riding in to Dallin single-handed gave him as much chance as a deserted calf ringed by a pride of mountain lions. He turned in relief to Mex who was leading his pinto out of the stable.

'That crazy fool Barrett's just ridden into town Mex. It looks as though we'd better take a hand.'

'Hold it,' warned Mex. 'We don't know the rights and wrongs of everything. If he's set on getting even with someone, he might have his reasons mixed. There's no call for us to back him up in what could be murder.'

Clint was in the saddle swiftly.

'We'll judge that when we see what's going on,' he replied.

Mex shrugged and hauled himself astride the pinto.

The spirited horse played up a bit just to establish the principle of equality between itself and Mex then followed Clint's horse out of the corral and into Dallin.

Barrett's grey horse was ground-hitched outside the Straight Flush saloon and just as Clint and Mex rode up, Leverson's big bulk blotted the light from the doorway as he entered from the sidewalk. They allowed him time to make his way inside then sprang up the steps and slipped quietly through the batwing doors.

There was a hush settled upon the usually noisy saloon. Tables had been vacated and most of the occupants were pressed against the walls. All eyes were on the puncher Colville who stood a little distance away from the bar and Mal Barrett no more than ten feet away from Colville and right in the middle of the aisle. Slim Murrow, who the pards had met earlier in the day, sat a short distance away from Colville calmly chewing on a cigar. He had a pile of chips in front of him. Marshal Leverson was inching his way down the aisle, gun in hand.

'I'm evening up the scores, Colville,' Mal Barrett was saying. 'We've played for big enough stakes in the past and you've given me no chance with your crooked play. I reckon I ought to treat you to the same but for the biggest stake of all you're getting an even chance.'

Colville had his eyes glued on Mal. If he was perturbed by the gun duel being forced upon him he didn't show it. Leverson's inching figure gave him a feeling of security.

'You've got things all wrong, Mal,' Colville replied easily. 'And driving me to fight it out isn't going to help you any.'

'Help?' snarled Mal. 'Who says I want help? You're the bustards who are clamouring for help, that's why you've sent for Shand.'

Leverson was only a yard away now and Barrett failed to notice that the attention of the crowd was on the Marshal.

'I'll give you five seconds to go for your

irons, Colville,' the youngster went on. 'Then I'm shooting you down like the coyote you are.'

There was a lopsided grin on Colville's face as Leverson's gun stuck in Mal Barrett's back, then the mark of amiability dropped away. Mal Barrett stood rigid while Leverson laughed harshly. The onlookers breathed again and some started to move away from the wall.

'Just take it easy, Barrett,' said Leverson. 'Reckon Shand's going to get his journey for nothing.'

Mal Barrett turned slowly, his hands well away from his six-guns and it was then that Colville went into action. As his gun cleared leather Clint fired from the hip. Colville screamed a curse as the bullet went through his forearm, sending the gun clattering to the floor. As Leverson swivelled to face the doors Mex calmly shot the gun out of his hand. Slim Murrow eased forward in his chair to get at his gun and Clint promptly shattered the bottle of bourbon that stood just in front of his face. He fell backwards clawing at his face that had taken a number of glass splinters.

The spectators were crowding against the walls again. Mal Barrett, quick to seize his advantage, drew a gun and rapped Leverson smartly on the head as the lawman grovelled for his own weapon then as the Marshal sprawled forward he moved quickly to the door.

'Beat it, you loco fool,' snarled Clint as the youngster came abreast. 'Get yourself a start.'

Clint and Mex gave him a minute while their guns held the crowd quiet. Blood ran down Colville's fingers as he explored his wound while Murrow's eyes showed they had escaped the splintering glass by the very intensity of the gleam of hate he cast towards the pards.

'Just relax, folks,' grinned Mex easing his lithe form back to the door. 'And don't come rushing out into the night unless you want a slug through the belly.' He motioned to the gunbelts he and Clint had dropped on the floor. 'These belong to Mappin and his herders.'

There was a quality about his smile that left the crowd in the saloon with the belief he'd enjoy putting a bullet through someone's intestines and no one moved until the rapid hoofbeats of the pardners' horses had faded. When the crowd flooded out of the Straight Flush, Clint and Mex were well out of range and headed on the Rafter K trail.

A mile or so out of town Mal Barrett waited for his rescuers and was busy taking the muffles off his grey's hooves when Clint and Mex drew rein. They glared down at him while he stowed the pads away in his saddle roll. He fastened the roll to his saddle and calmly built himself a cigarette.

'I reckon I owe you hombres plenty for horning in when you did,' he said stiffly. 'I guess I bit off more than I could chew.'

'I'll say you did,' grunted Clint. 'What you do is your business, Barrett, but taking your chance in Dallin with the law on your tail is plumb crazy. Do that again and you're on your own.'

'Look, Bellamy, I've thanked you for taking sides.' Mal drew deeply on his cigarette. 'But I don't remember asking you to side me and I haven't asked you for your opinion. I'm going to get even with Colville and a few more hombres in Dallin who seem set on framing me for a necktie party.'

'At the moment you've got just one charge hanging over you,' Mex put in quietly. 'Keep going the way you've started and they'll have plenty of excuse to shoot you down on sight.'

Barrett ground his cigarette out under his foot and climbed back into the saddle. 'Why don't you let me worry about that,' he grunted as he gathered the reins.

'It might have struck you that your sister could be mighty worried about the chances you're taking too,' said Clint. Mal Barrett turned quickly in the saddle and the expression on his face was hard.

'I reckon my sister would prefer to be worried over me fighting back than behaving the way I've done the last couple of years.' He shrugged his shoulders. 'Anyway, we've spent enough time palavering. I'll be on my way.'

Clint and Mex remained silent while Barrett gigged his grey into action. They watched horse and rider turn off the trail and merge into the darkness and after exchanging exasperated glances they set their mounts along the trail, riding easily, rightly divining that Leverson would have no intention of coming in search of Barrett by night.

When Steve Mitchell stamped up the three steps to the verandah of the Rafter K Stella Barrett stood by the open fireplace trying to ignore the rapid pumping of her heart. Now the time was upon her to refuse his offer of marriage, she was besieged with doubts and fears. Her face paled as Mitchell gave a knock and entered.

'Hallo, Stella,' he boomed as he crossed the intervening space to the table. 'Sorted yourself out?'

Stella gasped a bit at his direct approach and her eyes rounded as she searched in her mind for words. Mitchell placed his gloves and Stetson on the table and poured himself a drink from the bottle of rye that stood on an ornate silver tray.

The girl had changed into a close fitting green silk dress and the rancher was hard put to stop his eyes roving over her shapely contours. She caught one of his quick raking glances and crossing to the table sat on a chair opposite him.

'Well, Steve, I've given things a lot of thought,' she started, keeping her eyes away from his handsome face. 'And although I know deep down that I'd be doing the sensible thing by taking up your offer, I just can't bring myself to marry you the way things are.'

An ugly expression fleeted across Mitchell's features but by the time Stella looked up he portrayed nothing but concern.

'I understand, Stella,' he ventured. 'It's my guess you're looking at things from the wrong slant. You're a mite too proud to accept anything that smacks of pity and you're confusing my honest desire to marry you with an act of pity.' He reached over the table and held her hand in his strong grasp. 'I'm putting first things first and that means I want you for my wife. The Rafter K comes second and I want only so that you don't feel you're losing out on anything. The fact that you can stake Mal by selling the Rafter K is incidental.'

She looked up miserably. 'It's foolish of me, Steve, but when I give my word to marry I want there to be no other consideration of any sort.'

There was a long silence while Mitchell helped himself to another drink and sent half of the strong liquor searching through his tubes. He sat back then and looked at the girl levelly after raising his eyes from her heaving bosom with an effort.

'So you're ready to let Mal sweat it out in the hills with Shand gunning for him and Leverson ready to trade lead if he comes out in the open?' He made it sound criminal and Stella caught her breath. 'That's what it adds up to you know.'

The girl got up and paced up and down the length of the room, pale and worried. Mitchell stood up and caught her midway. He pulled her to him and gazed earnestly into her troubled eyes. His senses thrilled to the nearness of her and he had a struggle to keep the sensuality out of his eyes.

'Would it be so bad being married to me, Stella?' he asked.

The pressure of his granite hard frame made her nerve ends tingle and her heart thumped like a trip hammer. She had a tussle to bring herself back to the state of mind to deal with the question.

'It's – it's not a fair question at the moment Steve,' she managed to say, breaking away gently from his grasp. 'And I do care about Mal, you know I do. It's just that I don't want to marry for any other reasons than I want the man I'm marrying.'

Mitchell shrugged his massive shoulders with a resigned air and gave her an understanding sort of look before turning to the table and collecting his Stetson and gloves.

'Yeah,' he said. 'I guess I understand. Perhaps the best thing you can do for Mal's sake is to sell the Rafter K to me and provide him with a stake then take a place in town for a while where you can think about marrying me with nothing else on your mind.'

By this time Stella had regained her control and from somewhere deep the warnings flashed. She felt she should hang on to her home as long as possible.

'You may be right Steve,' she replied and now she was looking him straight in the face. 'But the Rafter K is my home and I'm sticking to it. I've a notion my new hands will help me keep it and get Mal clear from the trouble he's in.'

Hot blood flooded the rancher's cheeks but his voice was quiet and controlled when he spoke.

'That's fine Stella. It's always good to have hope but take my warning. Don't pin too much faith on those saddle tramps.' He assumed a softer expression before he turned to the door. 'Just don't forget if things get tough, head for the Lone Star.'

'I won't forget,' she promised and the smile he gave her at the door made her wonder again at her sanity in holding out. She heard him ride away then worn out by too much thought she made her way to bed. She lay awake a long time, too worried to sleep, and some time later heard the two new hands ride in.

The knowledge that Bellamy and his pardner were within hailing distance calmed her and very soon afterwards she fell off to sleep.

Steve Mitchell's first flush of temper quickly subsided as his agile mind played around the problem of the Rafter K. Stella's refusal of marriage had come as a shock. With Mal's chance of safety dependent largely upon her acceptance he had been confident that the night would have seen him home and dry. After mulling over their conversation a couple of times he shrugged his massive shoulders and dug into his vest pocket for a cigar.

When he rode into Dallin the town had gone to sleep but he ignored the saloons and rode straight down Main Street to the gaol-house. Tethering his horse to the hitchrail he climbed the steps and pushed the door open.

There was a pall of tobacco smoke lying heavily from the ceiling, almost blotting out the light from an oil lamp suspended above the table.

The four men around the table looked up and grunted a welcome. Marshal Leverson poured out a good measure of bourbon into a glass and pushed it across the table opposite a vacant chair. Mitchell dropped into the chair, tossed the spirit down in one gulp and pushed the glass back for a refill. He looked around at the others – Slim Murrow dabbing tenderly at his face from which glass splinters had been removed, Luke Mappin the trail boss and Martin Colville with his arm bandaged. They had their full attention upon him but characteristically he took his time.

'Waal, I guess we're through trading softly,' he said at length. 'Time's running out. I want the Rafter K signed and settled before anyone else shows up.'

'That suits me fine,' growled Luke Mappin, his face dark with anger. 'Barrett jumped my crew last night and drove off the beeves I'd claimed. Those newcomers backed his play and I'd sure like to take a strong crew in to wipe 'em out.'

Leverson grunted. 'I don't hold any brief for any of the hombres,' he said. 'But any killing that's going to be done had better not be traced back. Abe Ferris is due to make his rounds purty soon and he's nobody's fool.'

'Huh! Ferris don't see any further than the end of his blamed nose any longer,' Mitchell retorted. 'Anyway we can take care of him if necessary.'

'The sooner I can get square with that Bellamy hombre, the better I'll be pleased,' put in Colville and Mitchell glanced at him in surprise. Colville normally kept his own counsel about things. For the first time he noticed the bandage.

'What happened to you?' he asked.

Colville told him what had happened earlier in the Straight Flush saloon and Mitchell's handsome face took on an angry frown.

'Those two saddle tramps have caused us enough trouble,' he said. 'The next time they horn in I want 'em salivated.'

'Look, Mitchell,' growled Mappin. 'No matter what you've got in mind let's get it done. I'll keep my bargain but don't forget I've got a trail herd on the move and the sooner I get 'em to St Louis the better.'

'Your trail herd can wait until things are finished here, Luke,' announced Mitchell heavily. 'My boys have helped you collect every blamed maverick in that herd and you'll play my hand out to the last card.'

Mappin spread his hands then reached for the bottle. After filling his glass he looked up sharply at Mitchell.

'I want those beeves back that Barrett got away with and that's going to be my first move. With the herd out on the plains from here to St Louis, I'll get no chance to pick up any more.'

'Forget 'em,' Mitchell said as he took a cigar from his vest pocket. 'Slim will get word to my boys to run you off a couple of hundred head from Toft's spread. That's a durned sight nearer your trail herd than the Rafter K. I want you and your crew to make out you're Vigilantes and pay a visit to the Rafter K tomorrow night. Burn the place down and salivate those two interfering saddle-bums. Just make sure that Miss Stella comes to no harm.'

'Vigilantes, eh?' Mappin barely whispered the word. His attention and that of the others was fastened on Mitchell.

'Yeah – Vigilantes. You and Colville can whip up plenty of talk in town tomorrow.' Mitchell was addressing Leverson. 'So if Abe Ferris is curious, there'll be plenty of evidence that the townsfolk got together and took the law into their hands and burned down the Rafter K to smoke Mal Barrett out into the open.'

There was a long silence during which time the men topped up their glasses and drank deeply. Eventually Luke Mappin stood up and swept his Stetson up from the table.

'Right, Mitchell. You get those boys of yours to rustle that beef for us and the Vigilantes will be at the Rafter K tomorrow night.'

'Yeah, and I'll be right alongside you, Mappin.' Colville's eyes were hooded as he considered the pleasure of revenge.

There was a look of quiet satisfaction on Steve Mitchell's face when he turned into the Dallin Hotel a little later. With Stella

Barrett homeless and Shand on Mal Barrett's tail, the Rafter K should fall into his lap pretty soon.

CHAPTER FIVE

The next morning Clint, Mex and Hollister were taking it easy, perched astride the top bar of the corral fence, when McGraw's prairie schooner rolled from the Dallin trail up to the Rafter K headquarters. Stumpy Hollister dropped to the ground and crossed the compound to greet the wrinkled oldster who climbed down stiffly from the driving seat.

'Howdy, Ned. What've you brought?'

'Just the bales of wire you asked for a month back.'

Stella Barrett came out of the house and nodded to the driver. Ned Warren raised his battered hat, a serious expression on his face.

'Look, Miss Stella,' he said after scraping the alkali from his throat. 'I ain't aiming to scare you but there's a lot of wild talk going on in town about setting up a band of Vigilantes to come out and smoke Mal into the open. They reckon he's still here.' He paused to see the effect of his words but Stella was quite calm. 'I reckoned somebody

76

should let you know how things stood. It looks like there's precious few folks in town who remember how your Pa gave anyone a helping hand before he got killed.'

Clint and Mex heard enough of the conversation to make them come over to the wagon.

'Thank you, Ned,' Stella replied. 'It's nice to know we've still got one friend in Dallin.'

'Oh, that's alright, Miss Stella.' Warren shuffled awkwardly.

'Who's doing all the shouting, Ned?' asked Hollister.

'Seems to be Colville but that no account lawman Leverson is making it known that the law wouldn't interfere.' He scraped pointedly at the trail dust still lining his throat and Stella took the hint. While the men unhitched the gate door at the back of the wagon, she went inside the house to fetch a bottle of rye and a glass.

'Help yourself, Ned,' she invited, a half smile lighting her face at the gleam in the oldster's eyes.

'You're some thought reader, Miss Stella. I sure can use a drink.'

'Did you say smoke Mal out Ned?' asked Clint.

Warren paused in the act of pouring his drink to nod. Clint's expression became grim and he exchanged a significant glance with Mex.

'When the crowd starts talking that way, usually nothing can hold 'em back. You in any hurry to take that wagon o' yours back, Ned?'

The oldster gagged a little as he forced a mouthful of rye past his Adam's apple. He shook his head.

'No, can't say I'm in any hurry and I reckon McGraw'll be that drunk he'll not be caring when I get back. He sure hits the red-eye these days.'

'Good for you,' replied Clint. He turned to Stella who was regarding him questioningly. 'I guess they won't stop at burning the ranch-house down and there's nothing we can do to stop them. But thanks to Ned we've got time to get all the things you've got special feelings for to safety. Between our buckboard and Ned's wagon we could take a good size load of things to one of the line shacks. If they don't come, it'll be no trouble to move the stuff back in.'

'That's sound policy, Bellamy,' put in Stumpy Hollister. 'What do you say, Miss Stella?'

There was the light of battle in the girl's face when she nodded without hesitation.

'Yes – yes,' she said hurriedly. 'As soon as you're ready I'll tell you what to take.'

'You're a sensible girl, Ma'am,' put in Mex. He took the bottle of rye out of old Ned's proprietary grasp and passed it up to

78

her. She smiled at the look of dismay on Ned's face and came down the steps to refill his glass before taking the bottle indoors.

'If you fellers'll start getting the stuff out, I'll go and hitch up the buckboard,' remarked Stumpy and headed for the stables.

Clint nodded and went indoors closely followed by Mex. They went from room to room in Stella's wake taking note of the items she wanted saved and Clint's heart warmed to her as she made her decisions calmly without any visible sign of distress. Being practical, her first consideration was for provisions and they emptied the kitchen cupboards before moving on to the furniture.

They spent three hours loading up the prairie schooner and the buckboard and Stella worked side by side with them, helping to the full limit of her ability. She was flushed from her exertions, elated at the prospect of saving her best possessions and secretly pleased at catching some of Clint's unwary looks of admiration. She had discovered that Clint's stocky frame contained vast strength and his quick eye soon found the best and easiest way to manhandle anything. His cheerfulness made light of an event that could have been charged with poignancy. She found herself more drawn to him with each passing minute.

At last, sitting astride her roan, she watched Clint and Mex drag out a large box filled with ammunition. They wedged it into a vacant spot on the buckboard and Clint returned inside the house to fetch a couple of Winchester rifles. When he tried the mechanism before placing one in the buckboard and one in his saddle holster, there was such an air of grim purpose about him that Stella caught her breath. It was apparent to her that underneath the easy-going façade there was iron resolution and deadly ability. She had a feeling she would find out in due course that Clint Barrett was a lot of man.

After tethering Hollister's mount to the back of the buckboard, Clint swung himself into the saddle and frowned as his glance swept over the mustangs in the corral.

'How about those broncs?' he asked Hollister. 'I'm not aiming to leave any stock for the Vigilantes to kill or scatter.'

Hollister screwed his face up as he gave the problem some thought. 'There's a little box canyon a few miles further on than the Brush Flats line shack where we're headed. Plenty of good grass for 'em. I guess they'll follow that chestnut stallion if he's led.'

'Good. You get moving then. Mex and me will see to the broncs and Mex'll make a good job of covering up our sign. You'd better head out as well, Miss Stella,' he added, catching her eye.

The pardners watched the girl lead the way out of the compound and the big Zeeland horse that Hollister had hitched to the buckboard followed her as though its load didn't exist. Old Ned Warren's team were less inclined to move and he had to resort to some choice invective before the schooner grumbled its creaking way in Hollister's wake.

'That gal sure is spunky,' remarked Mex as he hitched his pinto to the post outside the house. 'And if I was the marrying kind, I wouldn't be looking any further.' He grinned at the swift look Clint flashed at him. 'Relax, Clint,' he said. 'As I said, I'm not the marrying kind.'

'What's it to me if you are?' Clint snorted. He turned his back and stumped into the stable to collect a rope halter before crossing back to the corral. Climbing over the fence, he approached the wiry chestnut stallion confidently. The animal's eyes rolled a bit and its ears flattened as it considered Clint, but talking all the time, the Texan got close without frightening the stallion away.

When Clint brought the halter from behind his back, the animal tossed its head doubtfully and a muscle on its withers twitched a few times but the soft talk calmed it and Clint had the halter in place in one swift fluid movement. The chestnut stood on its hind legs and pranced away its displeasure then quietened as the knot at the windpipe tightened. It followed eagerly enough when Clint pulled on the rope-end.

Mex unhitched the corral gate and Clint led the stallion into the compound. As Hollister had said, the other dozen mustangs followed behind the chestnut. Mex replaced the gate and held on to the rope-end while Clint climbed astride his own horse and secured the rope to the saddle cantle.

'Off you go, Clint,' the equable Mexican said. 'I'll cover up the tracks for a mile or so then join you. The sooner we get this chore done the better. I'm aiming to be back in that ring of cottonwoods when the trouble starts.'

Clint laughed. 'Yep, sirree. I'd kinda sorted that spot out myself. Mebbe the Vigilantes'll get one warm welcome.' He raised his hand in salute and kneed the dun gelding into action. When the rope tautened, the chestnut stallion went with him just to ease the pressure on its windpipe and the other mustangs followed their leader without hesitation.

Left to himself Mex employed all his skill in clearing away the evidence of their departure and by the time he quitted the compound, he had left nothing for an inquisitive man to find. An hour later he passed the perspiring Ned Warren and Stumpy Hollister.

'Miss Stella gone along with Clint?' he yelled at Stumpy then grinned at Hollister's knowing nod. He dug into his vest pocket for a cheroot and lit it carefully, cupping his hands to shield the flame from the hot wind that whistled past. The strong smoke drawn deeply into his lungs gave him an acute sense of satisfaction and well-being.

Mex eased his pinto's gait. He reckoned his pardner would welcome as long a time alone with Stella as possible. A slow smile spread over his face as the thought struck him that Clint would never reach the Llano after all. They had travelled a long way together from Butte, Montana, en route for the Llano Estacada where Clint was raised. Mex had tagged along intending to push on to El Paso to see his own folk but now he was willing to bet the lure of the Llano would not be strong enough to compete with Stella Barrett's undoubted charm.

He dropped back and rode alongside the buckboard, smoking contentedly and listening to Stumpy's vitriolic outbursts against Leverson, the citizens of Dallin, and the Vigilantes. Stumpy remembered the time when the Rafter K was strong enough to fight off any threat. It gave him no pleasure to be carting possessions around like a refugee. Mex sympathised but was more content to view things from a wider perspective. He was happy to leave stock-taking until the final card had been played.

It took another four hours before they finally hauled to a stop alongside the Brush Flats line shack. Clint and Stella had already arrived after having herded the mustangs into the box canyon some distance away to the west. The pleasant aroma of simmering coffee filled the air and Mex wrinkled his nose appreciatively as he dismounted. Clint was busy combing the dust from his horse and took time out to wave a welcome. Stella was attending to the coffee on the stove inside the shack's dark interior.

The buckboard rolled to a stop and Stumpy climbed down heavily from the driving seat. His full face was bathed in perspiration and he regarded the line shack doubtfully.

'It's sure gonna be some squeeze to get this lot in there,' he observed.

Stella emerged from the shack in time to hear his remark.

'Yes,' she agreed. 'I'm afraid it is going to be a tight squeeze. I was hoping there'd be enough room for me to stay here until the trouble's over. I didn't want to have to go into rooms at Dallin. The townsfolk don't seem to be all that friendly.'

Clint crossed over and grinned at her concern. 'I reckon we can let that lot stay on the buckboard,' he said. 'We can cover it over with those hessian sacks we stowed. Just take out what we need and that'll leave plenty of room for what's on McGraw's schooner.'

The anxiety lifted from Stella's face and she returned inside to pour out mugs of scalding coffee.

Mex unhitched the heavy draught horse out of the buckboard shafts while Clint and Stumpy took the strain to lower it gently until the tailboard settled, then while Mex saw to his pinto and the big Zeeland, Clint and Stumpy waited for old Ned Warren's team to arrive.

A couple of hours later the men stood back and wiped their faces free of perspiration after having stowed away the last item of furniture from McGraw's wagon. This time they had not permitted Stella to handle anything and she had sat in the scant shade afforded by the line shack watching their activities. Her attention had been for the most part focused on Clint. Each time the grin crossed his homely face, lighting it into more handsome lines, something from deep inside her craved for him and her heart hammered. She was afraid to think of the future and of a time when perhaps she wouldn't be seeing him. As she knew, footloose cowhands moved on. She wondered just how footloose Clint was.

'Well, Ned, that kinda lets you free now,' said Clint, breaking into Stella's thoughts. 'I guess you can get rolling back to Mc-Graw's.'

The oldster wiped some more sweat away and gave a sly grin.

'Yep. I guess so. Reckon old McGraw would have a fit if he knowed what I've been doing, although I don't think he's one who's turned from the Rafter K.'

Stella stood up and crossed to the wagon. She regarded the store driver earnestly, making him colour and shuffle a bit.

'Thank you, Ned,' she said sincerely. 'And thank you for bringing us the warning. I won't forget.'

'Aw, it's nothing, Miss Stella. If the other folk in Dallin just took time and thought a bit, I reckon they'd be plumb on your side as well. Anyways, I hope the blamed fools don't get to burning the old ranch-house down.'

He swung himself into the driving seat and gathering up the reins hauled the team around, heading them back towards Dallin. The others watched the creaking and groaning schooner until it was lost from sight behind a humped ridge.

'Mighty soft-hearted old coot, Ned,' said Hollister. 'He always was a mite fond of you, Miss Stella.'

'And a good thing too,' put in Mex. 'Or we might have been roasted tonight without a chance. The odds'll be a bit more favourable now. I reckon we'll get those Vigilantes in the light of their own bonfire.'

Stella looked up sharply, glancing from Mex to Clint fearfully.

'What do you mean?' she asked. 'You're not going to try to stop them?'

'I doubt if we'll stop anything, Miss

Stella,' said Clint, his face grave. 'But we aim to make 'em think twice before they try anything else on the Rafter K.'

'But there'll be too many for you to handle.' Stella's breasts heaved as she stared fiercely at Clint. 'You'll be throwing your lives away. Let them burn the place down. What does it matter? It's lives that count.'

A tender expression flooded Clint's face as he faced her. He decided he'd never seen a prettier picture of concern anywhere. He placed a hand on her shoulder and it reacted like an electric charge. His eyes were serious but sincere as he answered.

'Just don't worry, Miss Stella. We won't be taking any chances. But somewhere along the line we've gotta make a stand so that things get brought out into the open.' He gave her shoulder a gentle squeeze that made her lips a bit tremulous and her heart to pump even faster. 'At the moment we're supposed to believe that all this fuss is on the account of Mal having killed a gambler in what we know was self-defence. The sooner we know what's really behind things the better.' He turned away from her to prevent any other protests then swung around as a thought struck him. 'Have you had any offers for the Rafter K this last couple of years?'

Stella went red to the tips of her ears as she recalled Steve Mitchell's offer and the proviso that went hand in hand with it. She nodded.

'Just one,' she replied. 'Steve Mitchell has offered to buy, but he was only trying to help out Mal.'

Clint nodded slowly. It was pretty obvious to him what had gone along with the offer.

While Clint had been talking, Mex transferred a good supply of ammunition from the box to their saddlebags. They ate a meal of tinned steak, jerky and coffee then without further preamble they saddled up their horses.

'You stay here and see that Miss Stella comes to no harm,' Mex said as Stumpy Hollister made to remonstrate. 'We'll be back as soon as the show's over.'

Stella stepped from the line shack doorway and came close to Clint's gelding. 'Take care,' she said simply. There was a hint of moisture in her eyes.

'You have my word for it,' replied Clint then his smile spread across his face. 'My, you sure look pretty when you're worried,' he added before kneeing his mount into action.

For a long time after the pardners had disappeared over the hump, the girl stood gazing after them, the compliment chasing her concern away and setting astir her feminine emotions.

'Them's two mighty fine hombres,' remarked Hollister bringing her thoughts back with a jerk. 'I've gotta feeling they're gonna get us clear out the mess we're in.'

'Yes. We're lucky they happened along when they did.'

Stumpy had a flash of intuition and gave the girl a frank look.

'I guess they've been heading this way all your life, Miss Stella.'

It was a couple of moments before his meaning dawned on her but she was saved from commenting because Stumpy had moved away to busy himself with some chore.

The sun had gone down in a blaze of red and the wind had cooled considerably by the time that Clint and Mex rode into the ring of cottonwoods that stood raised above the level of the Rafter K ranch-house and outbuildings. Apart from the chirruping of the cicadas and the faint distant howl of a prowling coyote, a pall of silence had settled over the Rafter K. Light shone out of the big lounge window from the lamp Clint had left alight earlier.

The two pardners dismounted quietly, the well-oiled leather work hardly creaking as they shifted their weight and slid to the ground. Leaving their mounts ground-hitched, they removed their rifles from their saddle holsters and heaving the heavy saddlebags of ammunition on to their shoulders, they made their way to the edge of the copse where a fallen cottonwood promised to provide good cover.

They settled down behind the cottonwood prepared for a long wait. There was no need for talk. There was a deep understanding between the two men and no matter what danger presented itself, they had a pretty good idea what the other's reaction would be. Mex bit a chunk from one of his cheroots and chewed it quite happily while Clint contented himself by biting on a length of bunch grass.

The shadows deepened until at length only the lighted window relieved the gloom and vision was restricted to a couple of yards. As time moved slowly forward, the pards found themselves listening intently for the first sounds of the expected Vigilantes, then the tenseness would go out of them until the next time their senses involuntarily strained to pick up the tell-tale noises. They were destined to wait a long time and the minutes stretched to hours.

Every now and again they eased positions carefully just to keep the circulation moving normally through their bodies. When the time came for action they wanted to be in peak condition.

When at last they picked up the distant hoofbeats of many horses they were surprised that the sound did not come from the

Dallin trail but from the north. The oncoming riders were travelling fast and in no way concerned about the noise of their approach. Clint and Mex eased their rifles into position as the thundering hooves changed to an easy loping gait and again to a walking pace as the riders brought their mounts into the Rafter K compound.

A number of tarred rope torches sprang alight and the two pards saw a ring of about twenty riders, all with flour sacks over their heads with eye holes cut out and slitted for nose and mouth. Little clouds of steam rose amongst the torches from the sweating horses. The central figure urged his horse forward from the group towards the ranch-house door.

'Come on out, Barrett!' he yelled. 'Come on out! You've all got just till I count fifty to show yourselves then this place goes up in smoke. We're the Vigilantes and we mean business!'

The man's voice fell empty on the night air and the riders shifted themselves in the saddle as he started to count. One man shied something through the lighted window. The sound of shattering glass reached the pardners but no movement came from the house. The leader reached his count of fifty and the riders looked towards him for guidance.

'If you want to go up in flames, Barrett, it's your funeral,' the man yelled. 'Just send that sister o' yours out.'

After the man's voice died away the silence settled heavily over the scene. A horse snorted and shifted its position, breaking the tension.

'Damn you, Barrett! Send that woman out!' The man's voice held an unmistakeable note of concern but the silence merely mocked him.

A minute dragged by while the man sat astride his horse facing the ranch-house, a torch held high, then he urged his horse forward nearer the verandah and tossed the torch through the broken window.

'Burn the whole damned place to the ground!' he yelled to the riders. There was a pause then with a whoop they set to work.

The pardners saw the circle break and the torches light up the stables, bunkhouse, dining hall and ranch-house as the Vigilantes set to work.

CHAPTER SIX

'I guess now's the time Mex,' said Clint. 'Just one over their heads then aim to hurt. Those murdering coyotes are burning a woman to death as far as they know.'

'It's sure waste of a bullet but I reckon

you're right,' Mex grunted.

Their rifles spat flame one after the other and the men below with torches paused in their work before scrabbling for shooting irons. Flames were already licking out of the ranch-house window and the compound was taking shape.

Random tentative shots sent bullets flying over the heads of Clint and Mex. The pardners settled down in earnest and pumped round after round at the shadowy figures below. A tall flame spiralled out of the bunkhouse where one of the Vigilantes had spilled a kerosene drum over the floor, lighting up the scene, and the Vigilantes raced for cover away from the deadly rifle fire. A couple of them stumbled and fell in the middle of the compound.

From the corners of buildings already on fire, guns roared as the Vigilantes tried to silence the riflemen and bullets whined perilously close to the pardners, some thudding into the solid trunk of the fallen cottonwood. Then some riders burst out of the compound in two directions fanning out around the corral in an attempt to flank the cottonwoods and get to the pardners' rear.

Briefly the riders were lost in the darkness and it looked as though they might make it when the roof of the bunkhouse broke through and flames shot up high into the air bringing the entire area below the cottonwoods into bold relief.

Up the grade they came, firing their guns as their own handiwork robbed them of the cover of darkness. Clint took the left hand flank leaving Mex to deal with the others. The Texan's first shot sent the leader tumbling and the third shot made the second rider slump in his saddle. The other rider slid over the side of his horse and rode Indian fashion on up the grade and out of range. Clint could have stopped the rider by bringing down the horse but he could never bring himself to include a horse in a man's quarrel. The wounded rider had hauled himself upright in the saddle again but Clint saw him turn his horse round and head back slowly towards the compound. Mex beside him gave a satisfied grunt as the remaining attackers on his flank swung away back down the grade.

Clint reloaded his rifle and laid it beside his pard. 'I let one coyote slip through, Mex,' he said. 'Keep 'em busy and I'll play hide and seek with him in the cottonwoods.'

'I reckon you're a mite better with the rifle than me Clint,' Mex growled. 'You take over and I'll see to the prowler.'

The dapper Mexican slithered away from behind the cottonwood and Clint took up his position without a word. He knew that Mex was better equipped for stalking a man among the trees than he could hope to be for a long time yet.

Flames were leaping high from all of the buildings now and the Vigilantes in the compound had to vacate their cover as the heat drove them away. Clint was about to take his momentary advantage when out of the outer rim of darkness on the northern trail a lone rider came at speed for the compound. The rider was Mal Barrett.

Straight for the panicking group of Vigilantes came the rider, his six-gun blazing. Clint could imagine how Barrett felt and understood the fury that made him reckless to the point of foolishness. He sent a few quick shots towards the group and two men tumbled from their horses but he was unable to prevent them from getting Barrett.

The grey horse checked in its stride then stumbled, sending its rider flying to lie inert a few feet away from the blazing verandah.

Clint broke cover and ran a few paces down the grade, paused to fire at the remaining Vigilantes then ran down a few more paces. When he saw that the Vigilantes were gathering up their wounded, he held his fire. Then as they grouped to ride away one man pointed his six-gun at the still figure of Mal Barrett. Clint took split second aim and fired. The man toppled from his horse and the remaining Vigilantes spurred their horses away the way they had come.

Not wishing to be caught in a trap, Clint took his time getting to the compound but his quick ears told him that the horsemen had placed enough distance between them and the Rafter K to enable him to get Barrett to the cover of the fallen cottonwood before they could return.

The heat from the burning ranch-house was almost unbearable as the young Texan ran to the wounded man. In the brilliant light he saw the blood streaming down Barrett's face from a wound in the head and blood was seeping from wounds in the thigh and side. He grasped Barrett under the armpits and hauled him into the centre of the compound just as the verandah collapsed, sending burning wood splinters flying to the spot where the wounded man had lain. There he examined Mal more closely and discovered the wounds were not serious. The man he had brought down with his snap shot he ignored. He knew the man was dead.

Clint eased out of his slicker and rolling it up slipped it underneath Barrett's head, then after skirting the blazing, crackling buildings he crossed the corral and set up the grade for the cottonwoods. When he was halfway up two shots rang out, a split second separating them. Clint increased his pace although he had no fears for Mex's safety.

The blaze was penetrating the depths of the cottonwoods and as Clint bounded over the fallen trunk, he saw Mex coming out of the darkness. He waited for his pardner to join him then turned and looked back at the rapidly disintegrating Rafter K.

'I reckon the show's over,' Mex remarked as he searched for one of his cheroots. 'Those coyotes sure meant business.'

'Yeah, and Barrett came riding into the middle of 'em before they went,' answered Clint. 'He stopped some lead but not where it mattered. One bullet that grazed his scalp might knock some sense into him.'

'He sure likes to get in the middle of things,' grinned Mex, exhaling smoke. 'We might as well get our cayuses and take Barrett where he can get some attention. That's if he can fork a bronc.'

'I'll guess he'll manage when he comes out of his stupor.'

They walked together to where their horses were tethered and unhitching them, led the animals out of the copse. On the way they halted where a man's body lay at the foot of a cottonwood. Clint kneeled down beside the corpse and looked closely at the face under the flour sack.

'Colville eh?' he grunted. 'Seems you got the one who started the trouble.'

Mex nodded. He had already identified his victim. 'Huh, there's someone a whole lot bigger than Colville at back of this, Clint,' he said. 'I'm getting mighty curious to know what it's all about.'

'Y'know, Mex, when something big gets

going, it's a good plan to look first for the big man in the territory. The big man hereabouts is Steve Mitchell. On the face of things Steve Mitchell's a friend of the Barretts but it still sticks in my craw that he didn't give Barrett the defence alibi that night in the Straight Flush. One word from Mitchell then and all this wouldn't have happened.'

'C'mon, Clint, now isn't the time for palavering. We gonna bury this coyote or leave him for his pards to find?'

'We'll take him down and leave him in the compound alongside his murdering pardners.'

They lifted the dead man on to Clint's mount and walked the horses out of the cottonwoods and down the grade. They picked up another dead man whose face was unfamiliar and placed the corpse on the pinto. Slowly they transported their grim cargo down to where the dying flames ate away the last of the Rafter K timbers. Mal Barrett was sitting up fingering his head tenderly when they made the compound. He stared at them vacantly.

The pardners manhandled the dead men down from the horses and laid them beside the other man Clint had killed. Out of curiosity they turned the man over and removed the flour sack. They exchanged glances.

'Waal! The trail boss! Mappin!' exclaimed Clint. 'Now what in the heck makes a trail herder turn Vigilante?'

'Money,' replied Mex briefly.

'Yeah. I guess so. All we gotta do is find out who's paying the money.'

Mal Barrett was making an attempt to get on his feet and the pardners hastened to help him. He stared at them stupidly without any sign of recognition then looked at the gutted ranch-house uncomprehendingly. The blood had stopped seeping out of his wounds and was congealing in a healthy manner.

'Take it easy, feller,' said Clint. 'Let's get those wounds seen to then we can get you out of here where you'll be safe.'

Barrett regarded Clint woodenly then swivelled his gaze to the dead body of his grey mustang. The light of understanding came back into his eyes and his fingers went up to the raw wound on his scalp.

'You two eh?' he muttered. 'You sure came along at the right time.'

'Yeah, you could say that,' said Mex. 'It so happened we were here before you horned in like the blamed fool you are.'

'And you let 'em get away with burning the Rafter K down?'

Clint looked at him pityingly then shrugged his shoulders.

'No use looking at it,' he said. 'Let's take a look at those wounds and hightail it back to that line shack.'

Mal Barrett ignored him and staggered out

of their grasp to view the dead men. He took only passing interest in Colville but looked at Mappin, the trail boss, a long time. The pardners joined him and he looked up at them fiercely.

'The trail boss eh?' he gritted. 'Now how about that? The last time I went after his herd, I only wanted back what was mine. This time I'm gonna collect enough beef to pay for the Rafter K.'

'Now you take it easy, feller,' broke in Clint. 'The Vigilantes act outside the law alright but the law don't cross 'em any. If you go after a trail herd on account of what the Vigilantes have done, the law'll be dead against you.'

Barrett didn't answer but searched the dead trail boss's pockets until he found what he wanted. He extracted a thick sheaf of bills of sale. The one with his forged signature was on top. Stuffing it into his pocket he rifled through the others, then went through them again totalling the bills. He tapped the bills as he passed them over to Clint.

'There's near three thousand head in that herd,' he said. 'And if you take a look they're all signed to Luke Mappin. Mostly beef that's brought in by a trail boss is signed for on a company headed bill of sale. I'm betting this herd's been collected on a wide loop and every bill of sale's been forged the same as mine.'

Clint looked through the bills and Mex

100

peered over his shoulder. The trail the herd had taken could be traced easily enough. Starting out from Spring Valley with two hundred signed over from the Lone Z, it had crossed the heads of the Kiowa and Bijou Creeks, through Bijou Basin, past the little town of Godfrey, across Beaver Creek then past Pinnes to the east of Fort Morgan where it had entered the South Platte Valley and had followed the river's course. Twenty spreads along the route had contributed to the herd.

The pards looked at each other and Mex shrugged his shoulders.

'These don't prove anything, Barrett,' Clint said at length. 'But it looks like you might be right.'

Mal Barrett stood up and winced as the pain from his wounds stabbed at him.

'Right or wrong, I'm going after that herd and I'm collecting enough beef to pay for the damage to Rafter K property.'

'Well let's see to those wounds of yours and if you're in good enough shape to ride I guess we'll side you,' Mex grunted.

Mal Barrett took the pile of bills back from Clint and stuffed them into his pocket then sat down on the edge of a trough while the pardners checked and dressed his wounds. Both the wounds in his side and thigh were neat punctures where the bullets had gone through without striking any vital

101

organ and there was little danger of them rendering the youngster incapable of movement. The scalp wound however had gone a little deeper than Clint had thought and he shook his head as he dressed it.

'Y'know, Barrett, I'm thinking it'll be enough riding for you to get back to your hideout. You're in no shape to go after that trail herd tonight.'

The youngster lit a cigarette he had just rolled and grunted.

'Enough folk have said I'm thick headed in the past. I'm set on proving it now.'

His spirit appealed to the pards and they grinned.

'They way you rode in here tonight proves to me folk sure had you weighed up,' replied Clint.

Barrett's eyes moved around the compound and rested on the body of his grey mustang. 'Yeah. And it cost me about the best friend I ever had.'

It took him a long time to tear his gaze away but at last he staggered to his feet and looked around, screwing his eyes to penetrate the rim of darkness beyond the diminishing radius of light the dying flames afforded.

'That a couple of broncs there?' He pointed.

Mex nodded. 'You take it easy. We'll get one of 'em and transfer your gear.' He walked away as he spoke in the direction of the shadowy figures of two horses while Clint went over to the dead grey and removed the saddle and leather work.

Mex returned to the compound leading a rangy chestnut gelding that looked a cross between a mustang and an imported thoroughbred. Barrett regarded the horse sourly while the pards saddled up for him. He crossed over and ran his hands over the animal.

'You've got all it takes,' he muttered. 'But you'll have to be mighty good to make it a bargain.'

Both Clint and Mex understood the man's feelings. There is no partnership to equal that of horse and man. In the wide west they are of necessity inseparable and the years bring them so close together that the horse seems to react to a man's thoughts.

Barrett heaved himself into the saddle and after taking a last look at the smouldering remains of the Rafter K and the sparks rising high with the acrid smoke, shrugged his shoulders and gigged the horse into a trot. Clint and Mex looked at each other with an air of resignation then, grinning, swung astride their mounts and followed Barrett out of the compound.

They had been riding for an hour or so when a thin moon raised itself above the line of the eastern prairie. The light it spread was hardly noticeable but Mex found it sufficient to pick up the tracks of the departed Vigilantes. They lost the moon again when the trail took them along the foot of the Three Buttes, the bulk of mountains towering blackly into the star-emblazoned sky.

Barrett rode ahead, hunched in the saddle. Every now and then his hand reached up to explore the dressing the pardners had fixed on his scalp and each time he squared his shoulders in an effort to shrug away the pain. The pardners rode close behind him, ready to come to his aid should his condition make it necessary but he kept going with dogged persistence. They rounded the Buttes coming to the gap between the foothills where the plains opened out to the vast South Platte valley and where the strengthening moon shed a pale light over the leaning grass.

At last Barrett reined in his mount and rolled himself a cigarette. Clint followed suit while Mex lit up one of his cheroots. They cupped the lights and shrouded the glowing tips of their smokes with their hands just in case sharp eyes were watching.

'This is the end of Rafter K territory,' remarked Barrett quietly.

'Yeah, I gathered so,' replied Clint. 'This open range, eh?'

Barrett nodded then grunted with the pain from his head wound.

'Nobody uses it much. We've all got grass enough. Between the wind and the sun this grass gets scorched up mighty fast. That's why all the spreads hereabouts are on the west side of the hills. There's a belt of good grass in the river valley though.'

'We saw that on our way in,' remarked Mex. 'But that old river's likely to spill its banks anytime. Makes herding cattle there kinda chancy.'

'Any other spreads beyond those hills running north,' Clint asked.

'Yeah. Larry Toft runs the Lightning Flash in the big basin in the middle of the hills that run nor-nor-west and north. There's a gap a hundred yards wide, ten miles north of here leading to his spread. Lightning Creek flows through it and runs to the Platte River.'

'What sort of man is Toft?' queried Mex.

'All wool and a yard wide.' Barrett's answer came without hesitation. 'We don't see much of him on account he gets his supplies in Brush and favours that town for his social life, but he runs a good spread and I'd say he's as straight as a gun barrel. His old man was the same before he took his wife back east to live.'

Clint and Mex digested this information for a while then stubbed out the butt ends of their smokes and headed out across the open range in the wake of the Vigilantes. Mex rode ahead while Clint stuck close to Mal Barrett. Every now and again he stole a glance towards the youngster who rode with eyes tight shut and his face screwed into a grimace of pain. It looked as though Barrett would become a liability before the night was out.

They had been riding another hour or so when Mex dropped back. Clint held on to the reins of Barrett's gelding bringing it to a stop. Barrett unscrewed his face with an effort and peered at them.

'What's the matter?' he grunted.

'It looks as though a good sized bunch of cattle have been herded this way from that Lightning Creek gap not so very long ago,' said Mex. He rode ahead again and the other two followed. When Mex reined in, the others stopped. The evidence was unmistakeable. A tightly bunched herd of cattle had plunged its way through the tall grass, leaving sign enough for anyone to read. Riders had kept the herd bunched and moving. Shod hoof marks showed up here and there but horse droppings was evidence enough.

'Mm – looks like the Lightning Flash is gonna be short some stock when they get to counting heads,' Barrett said dryly.

'Could be,' agreed Clint. 'But we won't know for sure till we get to the end of the trail. I reckon we should do just that, then figure things out.'

Another half an hour's riding brought them close enough to the herd for the first sounds to reach them. Before this, Mex and

Clint had detected the acrid smell of singeing hide mingled with wood smoke in the wind. Barrett by this time was too bemused to be aware of anything but the pain which engulfed him.

When they stopped, Barrett pulled himself together and looked at the pards woodenly. He sniffed the air and listened to the bawling of the cattle then the light of understanding came back into his eyes.

'There's nothing we can do against a gang of rustlers, Barrett,' warned Clint. 'You stay here and look after the cayuses while we take a looksee.'

For a moment it seemed as though the youngster would demur, then he nodded slowly.

'Guess you're right Bellamy. I'll stay.'

Clint and Mex moved quietly through the long grass, any noise they made being drowned by the endless dirge of the cicadas. Unerringly they headed for the shallow coulee where men were hurriedly changing the brand of the herd the pardners had trailed.

Before getting to the rim of the coulee they lay flat on the ground and wriggled cautiously to the edge. Down below a dozen men sweated, roping and throwing steers, and a couple of running-iron artists added a box around the lone lightning flash on the fallen animals' hides. Another group of men were huddled around a second fire, attending to the wounds of a few prone figures. Some flour sacks lay on the ground just outside the circle.

'Funny mixture – Vigilantes and rustlers,' muttered Clint.

'Yeah,' whispered Mex. 'It looks like the Vigilantes are all trail herders. I'd be glad to know who the rustlers are and why they're doing the dirty work.'

They watched the feverish work below for another ten minutes or so then one of the Vigilantes crossed to the branding fire and spoke to the tall man who was obviously the leader of the rustlers. The two men stood in earnest conflab for a couple of minutes then the rustler turned to the sweating gang.

'That's enough, fellers,' he shouted. 'They say they can manage from now. Let's get going.'

Clint and Mex slid away from the edge and raced back swiftly to the spot where they had left Barrett and the horses. On the way they exchanged opinions and decided upon the immediate course of action.

Barrett was almost all in when they got back to him and made no protest when the other two leapt into their saddles and led his horse away without explanation. The moon had gained in strength considerably and riders coming out of the coulee would see them immediately, so no time was to be lost if they wanted to dodge a running battle against impossible odds.

About half a mile to the west they had passed through another coulee and without hesitation headed towards it. Clint and Mex cast anxious glances behind them until they rode down into comparative safety. When they reined in their mounts at the bottom, Barrett stirred in an attempt to ask what they were doing but Clint cut in impatiently.

'They were branding Toft's steers back there, Barrett. Do you think Toft will take a hand if we head for the Lightning Flash?'

Barrett groaned once then bit his lip. He took a long time in answering.

'Yeah. Toft'll let no rustling coyote get away with his stock if he's told.'

'That's where you and me are heading then,' said Clint. 'Mex has got some trailing of his own to do.'

'I – I hope I can make it,' replied Barrett with a grimace.

A few minutes later they heard riders travelling south and the pards relaxed. They had a quick smoke then Mex turned his pinto, and touching Clint briefly on the arm rode ahead out of the coulee. Clint took the reins of Barrett's horse and followed behind. At the top they parted company, Mex heading after the departed riders and Clint and Barrett towards the Lightning Flash.

CHAPTER SEVEN

It was near midnight when old Ned Warren drove his tired team into Dallin. He unhitched the schooner at the back of McGraw's store and stabled the horses, giving them a clean up and feed before making his thirsty way to the Straight Flush.

As soon as he pushed the batwing doors open, he sensed that things were not normal in the saloon. Men were still hunched over their cards, five women were going through a song and dance routine to the time of a piano, but everything seemed muted.

Ned saw that men's eyes were darting towards another group bellied up to the centre of the bar. Big Steve Mitchell, Marshal Leverson and Hugh Rolph the banker were there but they were dwarfed by the tall stringy man in the middle who faced the room. Ned pushed on up to the bar beside Mitchell and eagerly grasped the glass the barkeep pushed over. He gulped the drink down and nodded to the barkeep who grinned and refilled it. Only when the second drink was coursing its fiery way through his tubes did he take real notice of the man in the middle of the group. 'Shand,' muttered old

Ned under his breath and took stock of the man.

Shand stood a good six feet seven inches tall, his figure lean and spare topped by a face that was dried, gnarled and beaten by the weather and sun like some old mahogany painted parchment. A large eagle nose jutted over his tight thin-lipped mouth, vying for notice with an enlarged Adam's apple that went through an inch movement in his skinny throat each time the man swallowed. His eyes made old Ned shudder. There was no depth to them, just two slate grey mirrors that emotion would never touch. Above one eye a livid scar lay where his eyebrow had been, but whereas one eyebrow in most cases would add a touch of humour to a man's face, with Shand it only served to heighten the overall appearance of malevolence.

He was dressed sombrely in grey buckskin trousers tucked into black leather riding boots, grey shirt, black silk bandanna and a grey fringed buckskin coat. Although the night was warm he also wore a leather waist-coat. His Stetson, stained and battered, looked as though it had journeyed with Shand for twenty years or more.

The bounty hunter carried a long knife in a scabbard at his waistband and his six-guns were slung low on his thighs, the holsters thonged tightly to his stringy legs. The wooden handles of his six-guns gleamed from constant handling.

Shand finished surveying the other occupants of the Straight Flush and turned to the bar. His Adam's apple bobbed as he downed his drink and set the glass up for a refill.

'I guess you can ride along as far as the Rafter K, Leverson,' said Shand in a deep voice. 'And whether those Vigilantes have smoked Barrett out or not, I'll pick up the trail from there.' He paused to take another drink. 'If the Vigilantes did get to burning the place down then we might meet up with that sister o' Barrett's. I've sure got a knack of making little ladies give up information. She might save me a whole lot of riding.'

'You lay off her Shand!' Steve Mitchell's voice was harsh and old Ned standing beside him saw the cattleman stiffen in anger. Shand turned his head and let his pitiless eyes rake Mitchell from head to toe.

'Is it you or the State that's paying me for getting Barrett?' he asked.

'The State I guess,' replied Mitchell.

'Then I'll do the job the easiest an' quickest way for me, Mister.' Shand turned his head away as though dismissing the cattleman but he was watching carefully in the mirror behind the bar.

'You'll do the job without interfering with Stella Barrett, Shand, or the State don't put up the money. And if Leverson doesn't back me on that point we'll durned soon have another Marshal.'

Shand ignored Mitchell and looked towards Leverson. The Marshal gulped a bit then nodded. What went for a smile flitted on Shand's lips and he looked back at Mitchell. He shrugged.

'Reckon I just found out who's top man in his hyar town. However, from now on, every day extra that I have to spend searching for this Barrett hombre is gonna cost you money. You take away my short cuts an' I expect you to divvy up.' His eyes were once again raking Mitchell with the unconcern of a cobra and Mitchell felt his blood chill.

Mitchell nodded slowly and Shand grinned showing strong even teeth. 'You're a plumb smart negotiator, Mister,' he said as he pushed his glass across the counter. 'I guess you an' me will get along fine.'

Steve Mitchell grinned mechanically as he reached for his glass but his thoughts were a riot. This Shand was a mighty dangerous man to have in the middle of his schemes. Given the chance he had the ability and the gall to take over the town if it suited his book. There and then Mitchell decided Shand wouldn't get the chance.

The bounty hunter tossed another stiff drink down his throat then picked up his gloves from the gleaming bar surface.

'Well, Leverson, let's head down to that pokey of yours. I reckon those maps of your

113

territory will give me some ideas.'

Leverson gulped his drink down and turned away from the bar. He had no intention of keeping Shand waiting.

'You coming?' Shand asked Mitchell but the cattleman shook his head.

As the Marshal followed Shand through the batwing doors there was an audible hiss of relief from all sides and the noise swelled until the Straight Flush was back to normal.

Steve Mitchell stayed deep in thought leaning over the bar, clasping his glass of bourbon unseeingly. Old Ned Warren looked at him, mistaking his absorption as concern for Stella Barrett. He tapped Mitchell's arm and the cattleman looked around sharply.

'Oh, it's you, Ned. I hadn't noticed.' He motioned to the barkeep to fill Ned's glass.

'That's alright, Steve,' said old Ned. 'I figgered you'd like to know Miss Stella'll be safe from the Vigilantes.'

Mitchell turned full on to Ned.

'I don't know that any Vigilantes have gone riding, Ned, but what do you mean?'

'Waal, I had to take out some wire that the Rafter K had ordered today an' with the help of a coupla humdingers called Bellamy an' Juarez we shipped Miss Stella an' all the valuables outa the Rafter K to that big Brush Flats line shack. I reckon the Vigilantes'll set fire to a heap o' nothing.'

A deep scowl settled on Mitchell's face

then finding Ned's puzzled eyes on him, the rancher forced a grin.

'That was a mighty sensible thing to do, Ned,' he said. 'It's good to know that Miss Stella'll be safe from any troubles.'

'Yeah, that's what we figgered.' Ned made it sound as though he had been the prime mover but Mitchell wasn't taking any notice of him now. The cattleman had been banking on Stella coming into town after her home had been burned where he could have got to work on breaking down her resistance to his plan for the acquisition of her and the Rafter K.

Mitchell gulped his drink down and swore under his breath. He blamed the young Texan, Bellamy, for the breakdown of his plans. His crafty mind sifted around the problem while he poured himself another glass of bourbon and topped up Ned Warren's almost empty glass. Time was getting short. The Rafter K would have to be his before another couple of weeks went by. He was prepared for drastic action and his good humour was restored when a quick solution presented itself.

Perhaps it would be a good idea after all to let Shand frighten Stella a bit. A taste of Shand's handling with the threat of more to come might force her to agree with his plans faster than any other form of persuasion. He turned to old Ned and patted him on the shoulder then slid the half-filled bottle of bourbon beside Ned's glass.

'That one's paid for, Ned. Have it on me.' Then with a nod to Rolph the banker, he pushed his way out into the street. Ned muttered his surprised thanks and grasping glass and bottle firmly made his way to a table where a big-bosomed hostess who was fast approaching middle age sat resting her feet.

Mitchell made his way to the gaolhouse and pushed the door open. Leverson and Wilt Shand were studying a large scale map of the territory that hung on one wall. The rancher joined them.

'Maybe I can help you to a short cut after all, Shand,' he said. 'Barrett's sister moved out of the Rafter K today to the Brush Flats line shack. It's my bet that Barrett knows and he'll be seeing her.' Mitchell jabbed his finger on the map, indicating the position of the line shack. Shand checked the point closely and grunted his thanks.

'Someone spilled the beans about the Vigilantes, eh?' he mused.

'Yeah. I reckon it was old Ned Warren, McGraw's driver.'

Shand stood back a bit and looked hard at the map for a full minute. 'Much obliged to you, Mitchell,' he said at length. 'You ready, Leverson?'

The Marshal gave Mitchell a quick look then picked up his gloves and headed for the door with Shand. Mitchell came on to the sidewalk to see them off.

Shand's saddle horse matched him for size. Big, raw-boned and stringy, it stood a good two hands taller than the pack horse tied beside it to the hitching rail. The bounty hunter moved around the animals, tightening cinches and satisfying himself that everything was in riding trim. He fastened the pack horse's lead rein to the cantle of his saddle horse then rolled himself a cigarette while waiting for Leverson to show up from the stable at the rear.

When Leverson led his horse out, Shand ground his cigarette under his boot and hauled himself into the saddle. Leverson headed his cayuse up Main Street and Shand followed, ignoring Mitchell. The rancher watched him as far as the weak moonlight permitted with mixed feelings. Shand sat tall in the saddle, looking exactly what he was – a merciless, grim executioner.

Clint Bellamy pushed on through the night with as much speed as Barrett's condition permitted. Once he came up to Lightning Creek he was able to travel steadily in the sure knowledge that the shallow stream would take him on to Toft's Lightning Flash. Now and again Clint reined in to a stop and dismounted to check on Mal Barrett. The youngster was out cold but his pulse was steady and the Texan was not inclined to worry overmuch.

An hour or so before sunrise a cowboy came out of the gloom and hailed him. The puncher had been circling the sleeping cattle dotted around the dimly lit plain. Clint noticed the man held a six-gun in one hand.

'What's the matter with him?' said the puncher indicating Barrett. 'An' where're you headin' anyway?'

'I'm heading for the Lightning Flash – want to palaver with the boss Toft.' Clint rolled himself a cigarette and nodded back towards the figure slumped over the led horse. 'That's Mal Barrett, boss of the Rafter K. I guess he needs plenty of rest.'

The puncher nodded but kept his gun pointed straight at Clint's middle.

'Just keep on smokin' that cigarette, Mister. Don't make any moves for your hardware an' I'll take a look at the hombre you call Barrett.'

'Help yourself.' Clint placed his hands on the saddle pommel to indicate his acquiescence. The puncher eased his horse alongside Barrett's mount and after a quick look came back beside Clint.

'Yeah, that's Barrett alright. What happened?'

'Stopped a coupla slugs when a band of killers calling themselves Vigilantes jumped the Rafter K and set fire to it.'

'What's all that to Toft?' The puncher re-holstered his gun.

'Nothing maybe but the fact that I've seen about three hundred head of Lightning Flash steers rustled tonight could interest him.'

'Yeah?' The word came out slowly. 'I guess he would be interested at that an' if what you say is right, Larry Toft'll be headin' a war party before you've unsaddled your bronc.'

'That's what I reckoned,' replied Clint. 'Now I guess it's time to cut the palavering. Am I headed right for the ranch-house?'

The puncher nodded. 'You keep dead west and you'll hit the ranch-house about an hour after sunrise. You'll meet up with my buddy Mel Dodds at sun-up. He'll be on his way to take over from me. With a bit o' luck I'll get on that war party.'

Clint nodded and shook the reins to get his gelding into action. The puncher hauled his mount aside and with a wave resumed his slouched riding position. As Clint length-ened the distance, he heard the puncher singing to the contented sleepy cattle.

Just before sun-up Clint made a detour to avoid meeting Dodds. He had no desire to waste time going over his story with every cowhand on the payroll and he felt that Bar-rett needed attention as soon as possible.

As the puncher had stated it took just an hour after sun-up to make the Lightning Flash headquarters. Clint noted on the way

119

in that Toft's spread was a model of what a ranch should be. No broken down fences, no gimcrack buildings, everything neat, tidy and freshly painted. A throng of punchers holding their mugs of coffee lined the top bar of the corral fence opposite a big white-painted dining hall. The smell of coffee mingling with the fresh aroma of bacon and onions made Clint's mouth water.

The cowboys got down from their perch one after another as the Texan guided his horse past the stables and alongside the corral. They pressed forward to see who the wounded man might be. Clint just raised his hand to them and continued on to the ranch-house. As he dismounted two men emerged through the open doorway. They looked enquiringly at Clint, then their eyes switched to Barrett's slumped figure.

'Which of you is Toft?' Clint asked as he tethered his horse to the hitchrail.

'I'm Toft,' the taller of the two men answered quietly. 'That's Mal Barrett you're toting isn't it?'

Clint nodded and cast a quick look at the man. Larry Toft was a tall, whipcord man and although simply dressed in range clothes, he still commanded attention. His tanned lean well-formed features were dominated by deep blue eyes that gazed at the world fearlessly and frankly. His hair was the colour of old oak.

'Yeah, it's Mal Barrett right enough,' replied Clint. 'He's stopped some slugs but the only one we've gotta worry about is the head wound. I reckon he needs a lot of rest.'

Toft nodded and turned to the man beside him. 'Cut him down and bring him in Ben. Get Ah Lee to take a look at him. You'd better come inside, Mister,' he said to Clint. As Toft turned to go back inside the Texan beat the dust out of his clothes and followed him in.

'I didn't get your name,' said Toft as Clint crossed the big comfortable room to stand beside the fireplace.

'Bellamy, Clint Bellamy,' the Texan replied. Both men turned to watch three punchers carry Mal Barrett through the living room into a side room. A big deep-chested Chinese man followed them and Clint regarded him with some surprise. All the Chinese he had seen before had been undersized. A minute or so later the cowboys filed out of the house.

Clint rolled himself a smoke as Toft surveyed him quietly.

'What happened, Bellamy?' Toft reached out to a side table and poured a couple of glasses of rye. He handed one to Clint who muttered his thanks.

'It's going to take a bit of telling,' Clint replied. 'But maybe you know some of it.'

Toft motioned Clint to a chair and sat

down himself.

'I've got time. Go ahead,' he said.

Clint took a drink then started from the beginning. He told Toft everything that had happened ending up with an account of the rustlers and drovers who had been using running irons on Lightning Flash beef.

The tall rancher didn't say anything in a hurry. He sat with a thoughtful expression on his face for quite five minutes.

'Reckon you could do with a square meal, Bellamy,' he said at length and grinned at the look of surprise on Clint's face. The Texan had expected the rancher to make some remark nearer to the problem in hand.

Toft crossed to the door and yelled to someone outside. 'Bring in a breakfast for the visitor, Dan, and some of you see to those broncs.' He returned and sat down. 'Barrett's not going to be in much shape to hide out from Shand for some time,' he remarked. 'Reckon he might as well stay here.'

The man he had previously called Ben came in and Toft motioned him to a chair. 'Ben Holt, my segundo,' he said. 'Meet Clint Bellamy.'

Holt reached over and shook Clint's hand with a firm grasp. He was near middle age, two or three inches shorter than his boss and powerfully built. His face was rugged but good humoured and his gaze was every bit as direct as that of Toft.

A puncher came in with a tray of breakfast and set it down on the table. Clint's nose wrinkled in appreciation as the sharp tang of coffee drifted to him.

'Better get outside that, Bellamy,' said Toft. 'We'll go and take a look at Barrett.'

Without hesitation Clint turned his attention to the meal and the other two went through into the inner room. He had finished eating by the time they returned and was rolling himself a smoke. Toft held the bills of sale in his hand. He dropped them on the table.

'It sure does look as if that trail herd was gathered up without the owners' consent,' he remarked drily. 'But one thing's for sure, they're not getting away with Lightning Flash beeves.' He turned to Ben Holt. 'Take a look to see if Red Doolan's got back from night trick.'

'How's Barrett?' asked Clint. 'Any sign of him coming out of that coma?'

'He'll be alright. Ah Lee is as good as any doctor and he says that a couple of days rest will make him as good as new.'

'I guess that's fine then,' replied Clint. 'I sure wouldn't like to have to take bad news to Miss Stella.'

Toft nodded and his eyes held a faraway look as he pictured Mal Barrett's sister.

'You tell her, Bellamy, that if she wants to be near Mal she'll be welcome to stay here as long as she likes. She'll be a durned sight more comfortable too than in that line shack.'

'I'll do that, Mister Toft.' Changing the subject Clint tapped the bills. 'You're all set to get back what those drovers have taken from you. What about all those cattlemen? Looks like they've lost out.'

Toft looked at him in surprise.

'I don't aim to take on everybody's troubles, Bellamy. You should know a spread this size gives a man about all the trouble he wants.'

'I guess me and my pard could have ridden on out of Dallin a couple of nights ago and left Barrett to sort his own troubles.' Clint shrugged. 'But we didn't and we don't aim to leave until things have got sorted out.'

'You could have,' agreed Toft. 'But I don't get your drift.'

Ben Holt came back in before Clint answered. 'Red ain't showed up yet,' the segundo reported.

Toft nodded and turned his attention back to Clint.

'What is it you're wanting me to do?'

Clint blew smoke from his nostrils gently then stubbed out the end of his cigarette in the big fireplace.

'Now if I was in your shoes, Toft, I'd be taking that bunch of bills and heading for that trail herd. I'd take it over and push on to

Kansas City or Sedalia. Sell 'em at the rail-head, mail a fair price to all those ranchers and share the profits with the Barretts.'

Toft gazed speculatively at Clint for a moment then grinned.

'That's a mighty tall order feller. I reckon first thought folks would take that suggestion as plain loco. Now me, I like to think twice.' He cast a sidelong glance at his segundo who sat with a thoughtful expression on his face. 'What do you think, Ben?'

'It's durned good sense if we can handle the herd without leaving the Lightning Flash too thin. But I'd want to know the way of things from Barrett first, not this jasper. He might be planning on taking Lightning Flash stock while we're chasing shadows.'

'What've you got to say about that, Bellamy?' asked Toft, making no attempt to soften his foreman's directness.

Clint rolled himself another smoke and lit up before replying.

'In your place, Toft, I'd never quarrel with that sort of advice. Barrett's going to be talking in a day or so. I guess nothing's going to spoil waiting to hear what he's got to say. In fact that trail herd will be a mite nearer the rail-head.'

The segundo's rubbery face creased into a grin as Clint's sincerity impressed him, and Toft nodded.

'Tell old Barney to saddle up. I want him

to take a note in to Brush for Abe Ferris. I reckon we can wait for his sayso before moving. And send a few men to look for Red Doolan. He should have rolled in by now.'

As Ben Holt made for the door, Clint stood up.

'Well, I guess I'll leave you to it. I'll mosey along back to that line shack. Miss Stella will be wondering what's been happening.'

Larry Toft accompanied Clint to the stables, standing by quietly while he saddled his gelding. As the Texan made to lead the animal out, Toft laid a hand on his arm.

'What's your angle, Bellamy? Just where do you stand to gain?'

Clint's deeply tanned face broke into the smile that transformed it and his eyes glinted with humour.

'Sounds like you've never heard of a good turn in this territory. It just happens me and my pard have got time to spare, and no stomach to let a nice young lady like Barrett's sister get hounded and driven off her land by any bunch of crooks.'

The look Toft gave him as he led his horse outside and climbed into the saddle inferred that the rancher was more aware of Clint's angle than the Texan himself.

Marshal Leverson shifted uncomfortably in his saddle as he and his companion approached the smouldering ruins of the

Rafter K. He glanced nervously towards the lanky figure of Wilt Shand who sat bolt upright sniffing at the air as though enjoying the smell of burning that drifted down-wind. The bounty hunter had a chilling effect on all who came in close contact with him by day but as a companion on a night ride he was as awe-inspiring as one of the horsemen of the Apocalypse. Leverson didn't make the comparison but the cold implacable personality of Shand spread itself like a mortician's sheet and the lawman shuddered as he struggled to haul his gaze away.

Leverson had made some attempts at conversation but Shand ignored him, and they had ridden for the most part in silence except for the creaking of saddle leather and the background chorus of cicadas.

Wilt Shand was going through the period of initial elation that came upon him in the early days of every man hunt. His blood was singing through his veins as he pictured his quarry at the end of his guns. He hoped the man would grovel and plead. Nothing gave him greater pleasure than the sense of power derived from watching the terror in a man's eyes in those last moments before his guns, those supreme arbiters, silenced argument and reason for all time.

The elation would leave Shand after the first couple of days but in that time the resolve was born to see the chase through to the bitter end. The lust to kill was an insatiable mania and only the last twitching convulsive movements of his victim served to quieten his need.

The embers of what had been the Rafter K still glowed red in parts as the two men rode down beside the corral into the compound. They reined in a few yards away from where three bodies lay close together, and dismounted. Leverson pointed to the dead horse that lay a few yards farther on.

'That's Barrett's horse, Shand. Maybe the Vigilantes did your work for you after all.'

The throaty growl that emanated from Shand made the Marshal's skin crawl and he hastened to check on the dead men.

'Nope,' he said. 'There was sure some reception committee waiting for the Vigilantes. That blamed Bellamy and his pardner is my guess. Got clean away too.'

Shand looked down incuriously at the corpses. 'You know 'em?'

'Yeah. Luke Mappin, the trail boss – Martin Colville, Mitchell's sidekick and another trail herder I've seen in town.'

'Reckon I'll leave you to palaver with 'em,' laughed Shand gratingly. 'I'll head for that line shack.'

Leverson watched the bounty hunter sourly as the man walked to his horse, swung into the saddle and rode away. Without wasting any time the Marshal remounted and headed back for Dallin. He'd send men out in the morning to bury the corpses. As he rode through the night, thoughts kept nibbling away at his confidence. Since the coming of Bellamy and his blamed sidekick, the Mexican, plans were falling to pieces and the wrong men were going to Boot Hill. He shivered and drew his slicker in closer. The Marshal was no coward but he had a healthy liking for life and wanted considerably more yet. It took half a bottle of bourbon to cheer him up when he arrived back at Dallin.

CHAPTER EIGHT

When Mex Juarez left Clint and Barrett to trail the rustlers, he had no difficulty in keeping his quarry in view. Using every fold in the undulating plain as cover, he rode from point to point like a phantom, never once placing himself in a position where he might be seen. The rustlers took the route along the eastern side of the Three Buttes and where the black bulge of the mountains emerged out of the dimly lit plain Mex's task was made doubly easy. By climbing the steady gradient and setting his pinto along the thin deer trail crossing the shoulder of the first hill, he was able to get well in front of them.

A mental picture of the terrain flashed through the Mexican's mind and the image gave him reason to anticipate the rustlers' route. The first two of the Buttes were joined at the shoulder some two thousand feet up from the base but the third, nearest to Dallin, was separated from the other two by a narrow pass. If the rustlers intended making for Dallin then the eastern route would serve but if they were headed for any ranch to the west, it would be quicker to travel through the pass.

Having reached this conclusion Mex gave his horse its head, letting it pick its sure-footed way at speed across the face of the mountain. He was sufficiently ahead not to worry about being seen.

Arriving at the entrance to the pass, Mex left the horse someway up the mountainside well hidden behind a clump of mesquite, and settled down to wait twenty feet above the trail, stretched full length along the line of indentation where centuries ago a boulder must have rested.

Time passed so slowly that he began to doubt his reasoning. Perhaps after all the rustlers had hauled off due east of the trail. Just when his doubts were deepening he heard the first faint sounds of riders approaching and smiled with quiet satisfaction.

A few minutes later a dozen riders came into view round the curve of the mountain and stopped in a huddle at the mouth of the pass. A cloud of steam rose up from the horses and the acrid smell of their sweat reached Mex, watching from above. His sharp eyes picked out the lean hard figure of Slim Murrow the owner of the Straight Flush and a couple of men he had seen close beside Steve Mitchell on that first night in Dallin.

One of these, a heavy jowled, deep-chested man, riding high in the saddle, addressed the others, his words coming plainly up to Mex.

'Don't get to thinking tonight's work adds up to a holiday. All it does is to put more in your pockets. I want that herd in the low pasture shifted up to the summer graze. I reckon there's enough grass up there to take the whole stock now and you, Jake, get that bay stallion gelded. Mitchell wants him for the rodeo at Denver.'

'Only way to gentle that brute is with a bullet, Duke,' the man called Jake said but he laughed to minimise his remark.

'I ain't seen the hoss yet that you can't handle so get working on him,' Duke replied. 'If the boss don't want me for anything else I'll be coming straight on out to the spread so don't get to taking things easy.'

There was a bit of good natured chaffing and the party broke up, all of the riders except Slim Murrow and the one called Duke heading through the pass. Murrow and Duke

131

lit up cigarettes before continuing along the eastern trail towards Dallin. The tobacco smoke drifted up to Mex, setting up the craving for one of his cheroots. He had to battle with himself to let plenty of time elapse after their departure before satisfying the urge.

When he had smoked his way through the cheroot he gave a low whistle and his pinto picked its nimble way down the slope to him.

'Reckon we'll ride wide and beat those hombres into town, feller,' he said as he fondled the animal's muzzle. 'Just keep your eyes skinned for gopher holes.'

The horse's ears twitched together to prove it was listening, and when Mex mounted it stood on its hind legs to show there was plenty in reserve.

The Mexican's unerring sense of direction served him well. Instinctively he knew just how wide to travel so that he could not be seen or heard from the trail and he made good time to Dallin. Before entering the little township from the south end he muffled the pinto's hooves with the thonged pads he always kept in his warbag and rode in as silently as a wraith.

Dallin was as quiet as Boot Hill. Not a light showed anywhere as Mex dismounted and led his pinto between two store buildings opposite the Straight Flush saloon. A couple of pack rats scuttled from under his feet and shot across the dirt road but nothing else stirred. The pale moonlight carried enough strength for him to see clearly for some distance but the bulk of the store buildings made the space between as black as a cave and there was little likelihood of him being seen.

Thirty long minutes dragged away before Mex picked up the sounds of riders. He held his pinto's muzzle warningly in case the dozing animal might give him away, and waited with baited breath for the riders to appear. He heard the horses stop some distance away and for a long time there was a silence, then the sounds of footsteps grew louder as the two men walked down Main Street. They had left their mounts at the livery stable.

Slim Murrow and Duke stopped outside the Straight Flush saloon and although they spoke softly, Mex's sharp ears picked up what they had to say.

'Might as well come on in and get rid o' the alkali, Duke,' said Murrow. 'We've got nothing to tell Steve that won't keep till sun-up.'

'Guess you're right, Slim. My throat feels like I've swallowed most of Colorado.'

Murrow led the way up the sidewalk and after unlocking the private door at the end of the saloon, pushed his way inside. Duke followed and the door slammed behind them.

Mex gave them a few minutes to settle in and then led the pinto from between the

133

buildings, and mounting rode out the way he had come. When a few hundred yards away from the huddle of buildings he removed the muffles from the horse's hooves and skirting the town, made for the Rafter K trail.

He lit a cheroot and smoked with deep contentment. Things were shaping up. The night had proved beyond doubt that Mitchell was no friend of Barrett. The rustlers were Mitchell's paid hands and they were in cahoots with the drovers, who in the guise of Vigilantes had burned the Rafter K to the ground. Mappin the trail boss, who had stolen Rafter K stock on a forged bill of sale, had without doubt been in deep with Mitchell. The pattern of things was becoming clear. Only the reason remained obscure. Mex didn't punish his brain searching for that. In his experience the motives for double-dealing usually showed up in good time if one kept close to the central characters.

Before sun-up Wilt Shand had picked his way unerringly to the Brush Flats line shack and after checking on the number of occupants by noting just two saddle horses and one draught horse, made his way up the steep foothill rising fifty yards or so from the shack until he found a place that afforded cover and at the same time gave him a commanding view. A patient man when occasion demanded, he bit off a chunk of plug

134

tobacco and waited for daybreak.

When the sun's rays split the indigo skies he edged himself into a comfortable watching position and focused his full attention on the shadowy bulk of the line shack.

Before the blood red sun had cleared the distant prairie line a short tubby one-armed man disentangled himself out of a huddle of blankets beneath a loaded chuck wagon and after stretching and scratching for a minute or so, picked up a bucket and filled it from a ditch that carried a steady flow of water from a spring some way up the hill.

Shand had been filled in with all the details and had no trouble in deciding this was Stumpy Hollister. And with Hollister sleeping outside the shack it was dead certain that Stella Barrett was inside. The bounty hunter's Adam's apple went into its long movement as he mulled over the possibilities.

Hollister washed and tipped the waste water away downstream then after rinsing the bucket a couple of times, refilled it with water and placed it beside the dead embers of a camp fire. He raked away the embers and collecting the odd pieces of deadwood dotted around the camp, proceeded to get a fire going. There was barely enough wood for his needs so he went to the chuck wagon and unstrapped an axe from the side.

As Hollister moved from the wagon, the shack door opened and Stella Barrett looked out. Shand's eyes slitted as he regard her. Even at this distance the girl looked strikingly beautiful, and the bounty hunter enjoyed seeing the abject terror he instilled patent on the faces of beautiful women, almost as much as he enjoyed killing men. He gave a throaty gurgle of pleasure.

His all-seeing eyes picked out the rotting timbers of a juniper tree that had been split and uprooted by lightning some way beyond the shack. That was where Hollister would cut his fuel and the distance was sufficient to allow Shand to make his way down to level ground and across to the shack. A defile ran conveniently down the face of the hill and would afford him plenty of cover until, upon reaching level ground, the bulk of the shack would hide him from Hollister's view.

Stumpy rested the axe against the chuck wagon and carried the bucket of water inside the shack. Shand's evil mind gloated as he guessed the girl would be using it to wash down.

As Hollister took the axe and headed for the fallen tree, Shand eased his long frame to his feet and with the skill that came from long training, moved down the defile with as little noise as the passing of a rattler. Now and again he peered over the rim of the defile and when he was almost at the foot of the hill, gobbled with satisfaction to see Stella place a dixie of water to hang from a tripod apexing above the fire and disappear inside the shack.

The blows from Stumpy's axe were making enough noise to cover any that Shand made as he sloped confidently into the open. The three horses paused in their grazing to look at him and their ears twitched momentarily but the morning dew on the plentiful grass interested them more and they ignored him.

Shand came to a halt beside the shack and edged himself along to the end nearest to where Hollister would pass when his chore was through. He eased one of his long-barrelled guns out of its holster and palmed the barrel. Waiting for a victim was something else that Shand enjoyed and his mouth parted in a mirthless grin.

The axe blows stopped and inside the shack there was the sound of the bucket being placed in the most convenient place for Stella to wash. Shand swallowed hard in anticipation. His timing was just right.

There was silence for a moment or so then Shand heard the heavy breathing of the one-armed man as he approached the shack with his burden, Shand's grin widened and as Hollister rounded the corner, the bounty hunter brought the butt of his heavy Colt down with murderous force on the luckless man's head. Hollister didn't know what hit him. He pitched to the ground, his bundle of firewood spewing in all directions.

Shand turned the little man over, drawing pleasure from the sight of blood seeping out of the wound. He unbuckled the man's gunbelt and dragged it from underneath his victim viciously. Slinging the gunbelt over his shoulder he walked quietly to the door and let himself in.

The interior of the shack was dim. Stella had draped the window facing east with a blanket and it took Shand a moment or so to accustom his eyes to the gloom but when he did, he grinned evilly.

Almost one half of the shack was crammed with furniture stacked piece upon piece and a line had been strung across the remaining space with blankets and curtaining draped over it to make a screen for the girl. Sounds of water being sluiced on the other side of the screen told him that Stella had probably been washing her face as he entered and had not noticed the brief difference in light inside the shack.

He stepped lightly up to the screen and looked down at the unwary girl. His evil eyes roved over her until she felt the power of his gaze. She looked up and gasped when she saw the sinister face atop the straggly neck.

Her first impulse was to grab a towel to drape around her but she acted on the second. She darted for the chair where her gunbelt lay underneath her bodice and blouse – but she wasn't quick enough.

Shand ripped the screen away with one hand and swept a vicious backhand blow with the other that caught Stella flush on the mouth, sending her flying against a stack of piled furniture. She lay spread-eagled, staring up at him in wide-eyed apprehension.

Bad men she had known and seen but one who would treat a woman this way was something unpleasantly new. Blood trickled into her mouth from her cut lips and she sucked in breath in agitation making her bare breasts heave. Shand looked on licking his lips sensually then tipping her top clothes on to the floor, he straddled the chair to watch her.

Stella straightened into a sitting position, folding her arms but Shand leaned over and smacked her face hard with the back of his hand. The force of the blow made her gasp with pain and involuntarily her hands went up to ward off any further blows.

'Just keep like that,' Shand growled. 'Mighty nice shape you've got, Miss Barrett. I reckon a lot of hombres would like an eyeful of what I'm seeing just now.'

Stella said nothing. There was just nothing to say, but come what may she'd fight this man to the last breath. His identity dawned on her and she shuddered as she considered his reputation.

'The name's Shand. Wilt Shand. And I aim to get that killer brother of yours in my sights. You'll save yourself a lot o' grief if you tell me where he's holed up.'

'I – I don't know,' Stella muttered, licking at the blood that still poured from her lips.

Shand's big head nodded up and down as though he expected the answer but his eyes glittered cruelly as an idea struck him. He picked up the bodice and blouse from the floor and tossed them to her.

'Now there's two ways you can make him an' me meet up,' said Shand as Stella struggled to get into her clothes.

'One – you can tell me where he is an' you'll come to no harm. Two – you can stay stiff lipped an' I'll take you off, leaving a trail a mile wide for him to follow.' He paused, watching her attempts to tuck her blouse inside the waistband of her skirt without undoing it. Suddenly he reached over and ripped the skirt open with a vicious tug.

'No call to be shy with me, Ma'am. You force me to the second plan an' you an' me will have no secrets by the time I kill that murdering brother of yours.'

Stella's eyes spat fire as she glared fiercely at the inhuman specimen in front of her. If she had known where Mal was, she could never bring herself to say. She would have to risk the unpleasant possibilities that opened up for her but at every moment she would look for some way to bring this man to ruin.

'You're a brave man, Mister Shand,' she said quietly. 'Perhaps you haven't been told much about Mal Barrett.'

Shand looked at her puzzled.

'Wherever Mal is, he's not hiding from you. You'll find that out if you take me away leaving a trail to follow.'

Shand laughed but his eyes were thoughtful.

'My brother will outgun you and outsmart you wherever you meet and after what you have done this morning, you'll meet.'

'Regular fire-eater eh, that brother o' yours?' Shand grinned. 'Every hombre I've killed had been a fire-eater. Your brother's no different. Now cut the talking. Just head out of here and across to that gully. That's where my cayuse is stached.'

Flinging him a defiant look Stella walked to the door. His long feet lunged at her, sending her sprawling through the doorway to land in the dust outside. Tears of rage filled her eyes as she dragged herself to her feet, her face, hands and blouse covered with dirt.

'Just don't give me them sassy looks or I'll rip the hide off you,' Shand warned. 'Now get going.'

Stella led the way across to the defile and stumbled on up in front of the long-legged bounty hunter, coming at length to where the defile deepened and divided giving cover to the two animals standing ground-hitched and nodding in near sleep. She saw the rifle in the boot of Shand's saddle horse at first glance and without hesitation scrambled to the animal's side. Grasping the stock of the rifle she tugged to get it clear. Shand gave a bellow of rage and jumped towards her.

Stella fired as the barrel cleared, the bullet singeing Shand's neck, then he was upon her. He dragged the rifle out of her grasp, thrusting it aside, and smashed his fist into her face, sending her crashing against the hard, unsympathetic rock wall.

Pain and rage sent the girl almost berserk and she scrambled to her feet and hurled herself at him, clawing and kicking, but she was no match for Shand who thudded three more blows into her already bruised face, sending her to the ground.

Hard dry sobs welled up out of the girl as the hopelessness of her plight finally dawned on her but there was no pity in Shand. He stirred her with his foot.

'Get up, you goddamned bitch,' he growled. 'Take these broncs down below, get 'em watered and let 'em graze then set about cooking a meal. After that you an' me will take a ride.'

Stella dragged herself to her feet and did as she was told. There was a limit to defiance when the punishment was so drastic. On the way down and while she was busying herself with her duties, she railed against herself for having got into this mess. If she had done what Steve Mitchell had asked she would have come to no harm. She had taken the advice of the newcomers Bellamy and Juarez and now, in her hour of need, they were missing. Where were they anyway? And where was Mal? She regretted now having gone to tell her brother about the Vigilantes' intention to burn down the Rafter K. Her only reason had been to let him know that she was safe at the line shack. She should have known he'd go straight to the spot.

She gave a little involuntary shudder as another thought struck her. Perhaps Clint and Mex were dead. Mal must have come to no harm at the Rafter K or else Shand would not be here looking for him. The thought of the two pardners being dead was depressing but it was the Texan's homely features that stayed in her mind. She muttered a prayer that he might be safe.

Shand sat with his long back resting against the chuck wagon, his malevolent eyes following her every move. When she went to look at Hollister's form he growled at her: 'Let him be. Can't see that it matters two straws if he lives or dies. He's only got one mitt anyway.'

Stella fought down the impulse to give a scathing reply and returned to the fire to get on with preparing a meal. She was relieved to have seen faint signs of life in Hollister.

The bounty hunter was in no great hurry to move on and he kept Stella cooking until he had consumed a gargantuan breakfast which he washed down with four mugs of scalding coffee. The girl was unable to eat anything and the coffee brought tears to her eyes when it came into contact with her bruised cut lips.

During the meal Hollister stirred and groaned a couple of times but Shand ignored him and dared Stella with a wicked look to go to his aid.

Forced to sit and look towards the bounty hunter she was horribly fascinated at his animal appetite and the way his Adam's apple slid up and down his skinny throat. The man's overall evil appearance and the remorseless killer eyes made her flesh creep but somehow, sometime, she determined to find the means to pay him back in kind.

Finishing his meal Shand threw the mug and tin plate aside and ordering the girl to stand beside the chuck wagon, used some rope from the wagon to tie her hands behind her back. Then he gave her a push sending her full length on her face.

Stella steeled herself for what she feared might follow but gave a deep breath of relief when the man resumed his seat and rolled himself a smoke.

For a long time Shand sat and smoked cigarette after cigarette, then confident that his sharp ears would pick out warning sounds in plenty of time, he dozed with his Stetson pulled down over his eyes. He had been without sleep for three nights and needed a little time to recharge his wiry frame. The hot morning sun seemed not to bother him. The sun of many days past had dried all the moisture out of him anyway.

As he nodded Stella struggled and tugged at her bonds until her wrists were raw and every inch ached from the effort but Shand knew his job and she remained as firmly secured as ever. Hot tears of fury made streaks of white on her dirty face until at last she gave up the fight.

At length Shand came out of his half sleep with a jerk and slipped his Stetson back on his forehead. Every nerve of the man became alive as his instinct told him he was under surveillance. He glanced at his saddle horse and saw the animal staring northwards across the rolling plain. Its ears were strained forward and a muscle twitched on its withers.

Calmly he got up, crossed over to the girl and cut her bond.

'Get up and saddle up those broncs,' he snarled. 'We're moving out.'

He drew one of his long barrelled Colts and stuck the muzzle in her back. 'Just do what you're told and don't try anything. I'd blast your guts as soon as I'd kill a coyote.'

Stella nodded and went to do as she was told. She now knew without doubt that Shand would enjoy killing her. He was one of those perverted types who had never been able to fulfil himself with a woman and his loss had fermented a deep hatred of her sex that forced an outlet in acts of studied cruelty.

With agitated fingers Stella prepared the mounts for the trail while Shand stood behind the chuck wagon, his Colt following her wherever she went. She had fastened the last cinch when she heard the sound of hoofbeats and looked around in alarm at the grinning bounty hunter. She bit back a cry at the thought of Mal riding into his death and turned to stare at the ridge over which the rider would soon appear.

CHAPTER NINE

Clint Bellamy mulled over events as his mount's effortless stride ate up the distance from the Brush Flats line shack and smiled quietly to himself. Whatever the game was that he and Mex had stumbled into, they were keeping the scores even, and if Toft took a hand on the lines suggested by Clint, the balance of success would be in favour of the Rafter K.

As his mind played around the interested people who had been involved in the night's events, he realised there were others who were probably up to their own devilry. He was sure that Mitchell's burly figure had not been amongst the rustlers or Vigilantes and maybe Shand, the bounty hunter, had turned up by now. All of this added up to caution and Clint had learned all about caution the hard way.

While sufficiently far away from the line shack to be sure that his approach would not have been heard, he reined in and dismounted, then letting the lead rein dangle, ground-hitching his horse, he made his careful way forward on foot, bending low at times and sometimes bellying through the grass like an Indian.

Finally he inched his way to the crest of the rise that hid the shack from view and gently parting the grass, peered down. A slow fury burned up in him as the scene unfolded. Hollister was lying inert, Stella from the way she was lying beside the chuck wagon had her hands tied and the beanpole figure with the Stetson over his eyes, that must be Shand.

Clint checked his riot of thoughts and considered his line of action. The range was too great for side guns and a tracker of Shand's calibre would be alerted long before Clint got into range. Then the hunter would obviously use the threat of harm to Stella to save his hide. No, there was only one way to get in as close to Shand as he wanted and that was to ride in looking like a lamb to the slaughter.

He saw Shand stir, push his Stetson back then cross to the girl, cutting her bonds and Clint decided he'd have to move fast. Maybe Shand's instincts were at work.

Sliding quietly away from the crest, Clint made his way back to his gelding with all possible speed. There he unhitched his gun-belt stripping off the right hand holster. The gun he stuffed deep inside the waistband of his denims at the back, the holster he placed in his saddle roll. Then he refixed his gunbelt, thonging the one holster to his left thigh.

He rubbed dirt into the tell-tale thong marks on the right leg of his denims until he was satisfied Shand's quick eyes wouldn't know him for a two-gun man then he mounted the gelding and rode straight for the line shack.

As Clint rode easily down the grade, Shand moved out from behind the chuck wagon, his rifle aimed at Stella who stood at her roan's head with an apprehensive expression on her bruised face.

'Keep comin', feller,' Shand growled. 'And keep your hands away from your hardware.'

The Texan reined up alongside the girl's roan, placed his hands on the saddle pommel and looked coolly at the bounty hunter.

'Reckon you're calling the play.'

Shand nodded. 'Unhitch that gunbelt and let it drop, an' don't get to movin' fast or that Barrett gal gets a slug in her belly.'

Slowly and carefully Clint unclasped his belt and let it slide to the ground. Shand nodded his satisfaction.

'Slide off that cayuse and take a few steps forward, an' you, Ma'am, come in a bit closer.'

Both Clint and Stella did as they were told and as Stella halted some short distance in front of Clint, he saw the result of Shand's rough handling. He looked from Stella to Shand and back again, cold fury taking hold of him.

'Guess you ain't Barrett,' Shand growled. 'An' you're no greaser so that makes you Bellamy.'

'Right on the nail, Mister,' replied Clint. 'And what's it to you?'

Shand laughed a gobbling sort of laugh that made Stella's flesh creep but left Clint unmoved.

'My name's Shand, Mister. Wilt Shand, an' by my reckoning you've earned yourself what's coming to you on account you've been helping a killer to hide from the law.'

'Shand?' Clint mused. 'Never heard of you. What's supposed to stack you so high? You a lawman?'

The bounty hunter's grey eyes held no expression. They bored into Clint as he tried to exert his mesmeric will over the youngster.

'Reckon I'm stacked plenty high right now

149

Bellamy. You've heard of me alright. Wilt Shand – bounty hunter, an' that gives me plenty o' weight with the law when I tell 'em I had to kill you when you jumped me at the line shack.'

Clint nodded slowly and jerked his head towards Stella who stood with her hand to her throat.

'You do that, Shand?'

The bounty hunter eased one of his long barrelled Colts into his right hand and let the rifle drop.

'Yeah. She got sassy. Never could abide a sassy woman, Bellamy. It ain't nothing to what she's goin' to get before I'm through with her though. Still, you ain't goin' to be around so it's no skin off your nose.'

'Mighty spunky hombre eh?' Clint gave a tight laugh. 'Regular fire-eater! Ever tried doling out that treatment to a man?'

Shand dismissed the question with a shrug.

'Five minutes from now, Bellamy, me an' that sassy bitch'll be riding out from here. You won't be coming so I'll have to salivate you.'

Clint caught the agonised expression on Stella's face and felt savage satisfaction in the pain the barrel of his Colt gave him in the small of his back. He shrugged away Shand's words as though disbelieving.

'Time for a smoke then eh, Shand?'

The bounty hunter nodded, his Adam's

apple starting to slide up and down in anticipation of a killing.

Slowly Clint pulled out the makings and rolled a cigarette with fingers as steady as a rock. He returned the makings and searched for matches. Failing to find them by patting his shirt pockets, he reached around to his right hand back pocket. Shand was watching him closely but unsuspecting. The Texan's hand closed over the butt of his Colt and it came away easily.

In a blur of movement Clint slipped sideways, his gun roaring twice. The first bullet sent Shand's long barrelled Colt flying out of his hand, the second smashed the butt of the other Colt in the bounty hunter's holster. Stella screamed, not being certain who had fired the first shot then laughed hysterically as she realised Clint was safe.

For a moment Shand stared in disbelief at the stocky Texan who had outwitted him and the madness of the man welled up. Disregarding the gun the advancing Clint held, he darted to regain possession of his rifle but he was too late. The Texan leapt in and stepped on the man's clawing hands then kicked the rifle well out of reach. Shand lay full stretch, his face upturned towards Clint, murder plain on every feature. Clint stood back and glared contemptuously at the woman beater.

'Get up, Shand, and make it fast or I'll drill you right now.'

Clint heard Stella gasp but he was in no mood to be squeamish on a woman's account.

'You, Stella,' he yelled. 'Grab a gun then take a look at Hollister. Mebbe you can do something for him.'

Shand came slowly to his feet, his long thin frame shrinking from the Texan's malevolent gaze. He backed away until he came against the tail of the chuck wagon.

'Now you take it easy, Bellamy,' he gabbled. 'I'm just ahead of the law. They're gonna be on your tail mighty soon if anything happens to me.'

Clint's right hand connected with the bounty hunter's jaw stopping the flow of words. Stella paused in the act of crossing to Hollister to watch. The air of bleak purpose about the Texan as he closed in spread confidence in her and she gave her attention to the still unconscious Hollister.

The first blow from Clint cleared away the surprise and the first faint touch of fear that clutched at Shand's heart. Tough as a timber wolf, he towered over the Texan and chopped vicious blows at him but Clint evaded them easily and thumped his fist deep into the man's stomach.

Shand tried bringing his knee into play and Clint slipped out of distance just in time. The bounty hunter seized the brief respite to dive for the rifle a few feet away.

As his hand closed over the stock Clint was on top of him. They rolled, locked together, flailing blows and gouging each other, the killer instinct riding high. Inexorably the strength of the younger man dictated the way of things. Shand's blows carried less and less power as the fight went on whilst Clint's sledge hammer fists thudded into him with unabated ferocity.

Clint could feel Shand weakening but there was no pity in him. He thumped two solid rights flush on the man's prominent Adam's apple and saw Shand's eyelids flutter. He jumped to his feet and dragged the bounty hunter's length upright. Holding him with one hand, he smashed punches into him with the other.

Long after the power to resist had drained from Shand, Clint went to work on him. Minutes later when he relaxed his grasp on the man's shirt: what slipped to the ground was a shell. The spirit and spunk had been pummelled out of him for all time.

Clint gazed at his skinned knuckles in a dazed sort of way. Sweat streamed from him and he drew deep breaths into his heaving chest. He crossed into the line shack, conscious that Stella's eyes followed him and finding a length of rope, returned to Shand's battered body. Carefully he bound the bounty hunter and picking him up without ceremony, dragged him under the chuck wagon and returned into the sunshine. He mopped at his face with a bandanna and walked over to where Stella was bathing Hollister's wound. He crouched down and regarded her thoughtfully. The girl looked up sharply, her eyes bright with tears of relief.

'I – I'll never be able to thank you enough. That man is a fiend.'

Clint smiled but changed the subject. He nodded to Hollister's still figure.

'How is he?'

'He's breathing steadily enough. I think he'll come out of it soon.'

Clint examined the deep wound carefully. It was a nasty gash but he had seen worse. He collected some water from the stream and bandages from his warbag and helped Stella to clean and bind the wound. As they drew near together ministering to the injured man, they each felt the magnetism of the other. Their hands touched and their attention wavered from Hollister only to return as the man groaned.

Stumpy's eyes flickered open, closed again in pain then re-opened. After a grimace he grinned up at Stella.

'What in heck hit me?' he asked.

Clint stood up, glad of an excuse to do something. The nearness of the girl was disturbing and he wasn't sure that any good would come from his feelings for her. When he rode away from Dallin for the last time,

154

he wanted to ride light of heart.

'I'll see to my cayuse then I guess I'll grab some shuteye,' he said briefly. Stella stood up and held on to his arm as he moved away. Her eyes held his and there was a depth of feeling in them that made his blood run hot.

'You must be worn out,' she said. 'I'll cook a meal for you before you sleep.' She nodded towards Stumpy who was now sitting up. 'I guess a good meal will do him some good too.'

There were questions she wanted to ask but she didn't press him for news. She had sufficient insight to know he would tell her everything at the right time.

A little later Clint sat down beside Hollister to eat the meal prepared by Stella. Stumpy was still a bit dazed but he was made of tough material and Clint was satisfied he would soon recover completely. Stella had washed herself at the stream but although the dirt had been removed from her face, the dark bruises still showed where Shand's blows had struck her. She helped herself to a mug of coffee and sat opposite the two men. Clint looked up and smiled.

'I guess you'd like to know Mal is resting up at Toft's spread,' he said. 'He stopped a couple of slugs riding in on the Vigilantes but there's nothing to worry about. Just a couple of flesh wounds an' one that skimmed his scalp. He'll be as good as new in a few days. Toft says you're welcome to stay at the Lightning Flash while Mal recuperates.' He set his plate down and reached for his mug of coffee. 'The Vigilantes did just like they said. I reckon we'll have to build another Rafter K.'

There were tears in Stella's eyes as she pictured the ruin of what had been her home for so long but she shrugged them away as she realised how little Clint had told her of the night's events. If Mal had been wounded riding into the Rafter K while the Vigilantes had been busy, then the Texan and his pardner must have taken grim chances to save him. She looked at Clint's stocky solid frame and her heart warmed to him.

'I'll stay here, Clint,' she said simply.

The youngster looked up sharply. She used his name as though it meant something and the flush that stole up her neck gave emphasis to his belief. He nodded, trying to fight down the mounting excitement generated by his thoughts.

'Yeah, it's my guess you'll be as safe here as anywhere now that Shand's teeth have been drawn,' he replied briefly. 'And I reckon Mal will be on his feet before you'd make the Lightning Flash anyway.'

He went on to tell Stella and Hollister who the Vigilantes had been and about the men who had rustled Lightning Flash stock. He was concluding by recounting the plan for Toft to take over the trail herd when Mex rode in.

The Mexican's sharp eyes spotted Shand's trussed form under the chuck wagon, Hollister's wound and the bruises on Stella's face. He had pieced the story together before he unsaddled his horse.

'That the bounty hunter?' he asked, indicating Shand. Clint nodded and Mex grinned. 'Got plenty mad at him eh?' His eyes sneaked a glance at Stella's face and Clint flushed. 'What are you gonna do with him?'

'Might tote him into Dallin. It'll mebbe let 'em know the Rafter K can hit back.'

Mex considered this and looked again at Stella's face.

'Can't see why we should let him get out with a whole skin,' he said smoothly. 'Let's see if he's as fast on the draw as his reputation says.'

Clint shook his head firmly. 'Nope. It'll hurt him a lot more having to live down failure. Anyway, Toft who runs the Lightning Flash spread has sent to Brush for Abe Ferris, the Sheriff. I reckon we'll let Ferris decide what to do with him.'

Whilst Mex ate, they exchanged information. At the mention of the link between the rustlers and Steve Mitchell, Stella jumped up, her eyes probing the Mexican's enigmatic gaze.

'You must be mistaken,' she said. 'Steve Mitchell has been a friend for a long time and I can't believe he's mixed up with rustling or anything outside the law.'

'He's the one who's trying to buy up the Rafter K, isn't he?' Clint gave her a cool look as he spoke. The way she flew in defence of Mitchell irritated him. 'I reckon if we knew why he wanted your spread, we'd have the answers to a lot of things.'

Stella flushed hotly as she considered what Mitchell had wanted along with the Rafter K. Clint mistook her emotion as concern for Mitchell and he stood up, a dour expression on his face.

'I'll get some shut-eye. Reckon I'll sleep till sundown.' He stomped off towards the line shack, first checking on Shand.

Stella watched him go, a puzzled expression on her face. Hollister winced as he nodded towards Clint.

'What in heck's got into him?' he asked.

Stella shrugged her shoulders but Mex laughed aloud and cast a knowing glance at the girl. She made a great play of cleaning up the dishes and Mex, still grinning, got up and followed Clint.

The two pards slept until well after sundown. Both were as hard as iron and well able to stand up to long arduous journeys with only brief snatches of sleep but when

the opportunity presented itself they revital-
ised themselves by complete and long
relaxation. They had been without sleep for
almost three days and this seemed a good
time to catch up.

Hollister was standing in front of Shand,
holding a six-gun and watching the bounty
hunter eat up the remains of a meal. Stella
stood beside Hollister waiting to tie Shand
up again. Mex crossed over to them but Clint
walked to the fire and helped himself to a
mug of coffee. Stella joined him after a while
and busied herself cooking a meal. Now and
again she stole glances at the Texan's stocky
figure but Clint remained sitting quietly gazing into the fire and sipping the scalding
coffee.

The girl knew instinctively that her apparent defence of Mitchell was responsible for
Clint's aloofness and she searched in her
mind for a way to impress him that her
concern for Mitchell was only that of a friend
of long standing, but he gave no indication
that he wanted to talk and as the minutes
passed away, a wall of resentment began to
build up in her. Why should she have to
explain herself to him? Her indignation grew
until when the others joined them around the
fire, she was hard of face and morose.

Without a word she gave them each their
plates, then taking her own and a mug of
coffee walked away to the shack. Hollister

159

looked after her in surprise but Mex affected not to notice. The three men finished their meal and smoked a cigarette apiece while they yarned in the inimitable manner of the plainsman. Stella did not re-appear and at length Hollister turned into his bed on the chuck wagon. Mex and Clint took turns throughout the night to keep guard and check on the bounty hunter.

Shand was awake through most of the night but never once did he utter a word. His eyes mirrored the pale light of the moon each time the pardners looked at him but the glitter of deep venomous hate was in them. The beating he had taken had washed away the confidence that would allow him to ride in upon a man ready to take his chance but his hate for the young Texan was such that his mind was filled with the desire for revenge. If it was the last thing he did, he'd ambush Bellamy and leave him for the buzzards.

CHAPTER TEN

It was the following morning that Mal Barrett woke up clearheaded and completely free from the effects of the wound in his scalp. He looked up in some surprise at Ah Lee, Toft's massive cook and general factotum, who

160

grinned at him from beside the bed. He shut his eyes again and kept them closed while his memory brought him up to date.

'How long have I been here, Ah Lee?' he asked at length.

'Two days, Mister Barrett,' replied the Chinaman. 'Me tell Mister Toft you ready to talk to him.' Before leaving the room, he placed some cigarettes on a table beside the bed and Barrett reached out and took one.

A few minutes later Larry Toft came in together with Ben Holt. Mal nodded to them and winced at the pain caused by the sudden movement.

'How are you feeling, Barrett?' asked Toft as he straddled the chair beside the bed. Holt sat on the end of the bed.

'I guess I'm alright now. It's mighty good of you to have taken me in considering I'm on the dodge.'

Toft laughed. 'I don't go much on Vigilantes and bounty hunters, Mal, and anyway I'm ready to take your sayso how that gambler died. Bellamy tells me he went for his shooting iron first and if that's your story, I'm not worried what Leverson says. You've been a blamed fool for a long time but I reckon your word stands up one hundred per cent.'

'That's the way it happened, Larry,' Mal answered. 'But I'm not doing any running. Someone stirred up feeling to get those Vigilantes to burn down the Rafter K and

161

I'm going to find out who.'

'You'd better hold your horses, Barrett,' put in Ben Holt. 'Abe Ferris'll be here mighty soon. I'd let him handle things.'

Mal looked at the two men sharply. He took another cigarette, a thoughtful expression on his face.

'If Ferris is on his way, I guess I'll be moving on. Abe's a mighty good lawman and a straight shooter but he might back Leverson's play just to get me out of Shand's way. Nope, I want to be free to hit back at the bustards who've planned to rub out the Rafter K.'

Ah Lee came in at that moment with a tray of breakfast. Toft moved out of the way and he placed the tray in front of Barrett.

'Looks mighty good, Ah Lee,' said Mal. 'You're blamed lucky to have a man like Ah Lee around,' he added to Toft. The Chinese bowed in acknowledgment and looked suitably gratified as he went out.

While Barrett ate heartily, Toft told him about Bellamy's idea to take over the trail herd. Mal listened with increasing interest.

'That Bellamy sure has bright ideas. You going to act on it, Larry?'

'I guess that depends on what Abe Ferris has got to say. If he agrees, Ben will take all the men we can spare and do battle for the herd. In any case we're taking back our stock.'

162

'I'd like to lend a hand but I'm aiming to hit the trail before Ferris gets here,' said Mal. 'I sure hope you get all the luck, Ben.'

The segundo's face was grim as he considered the job he might be expected to tackle. It was a tough assignment but he was a mighty tough man.

'Luck don't play much part in my reckoning,' he said flatly. 'If Ferris gives the all clear, I'll take that herd as sure as Hades.'

Mal nodded and placed the empty tray on the table beside the bed. He threw back the covers and stepped on to the floor. His head stood the test alright but there was a soreness about his other flesh wounds that suggested he'd do better to rest up a while. He shrugged the thought away and reached for his clothes. Neither Toft nor Holt tried to dissuade him, being of the opinion he was man enough to know his own mind. A short time later he rode away towards Dallin.

'Reckon he'd have done better to wait for Ferris, Ben,' said Toft as Barrett rode out of sight.

'Don't know that I agree,' replied the segundo. 'He's fooled about plenty in the past. The only way he'll get some iron inside him is by playing things out the way he sees 'em.'

Toft was used to Holt's sage remarks. He himself had leaned a lot on his segundo in his younger days.

'Huh. You're mebbe right at that,' he answered before giving his attention to ranch details.

When Stella awoke the next morning she emerged from the line shack to find Clint and Mex saddled up ready for the trail. They were busy trussing the skinny silent bounty hunter to his saddle horse. She crossed to the fire and Stumpy Hollister handed her a mug of coffee with a welcoming grin. She looked mechanically from him to the pardners.

'Where are they going?' Then in an apologetic tone for not having asked about the state of his health first: 'And how do you feel today?'

'Oh I'm alright now I guess, Miss Stella,' Hollister replied. 'They're taking Shand to the Lightning Flash to let Abe Ferris deal with him for what he did to you.'

A couple of minutes later Clint and Mex mounted their horses. Mex gave Stella and Hollister a cheery wave as they rode out leading Shand's saddle horse and pack animal but Clint looked straight ahead. As they came abreast Clint barked an instruction at Hollister.

'Keep your shooting iron handy an' don't wander away from camp.'

'You betcha, Clint,' the oldster promised. 'Nobody's gonna jump me a second time.'

Stella watched them go and her lower lip

trembled a little at Clint's unbending behaviour. Her temper of the previous night had softened with sleep and she had hoped that Clint would have recovered his good humour by the morning. She felt an unaccountable heaviness of the heart at the rift that had come between them just when their understanding was set to deepen.

Hollister prepared breakfast and Stella ate mechanically, absorbed in the oldest of women's problems, how to impress the man you want that you love him without appearing too forward. Hollister watched her from under his thick brows.

'That Bellamy sure seems to have something on his mind,' he remarked for no apparent reason.

Stella looked at him sharply. 'What do you mean?' she asked.

'He acts as though he's gonna make a mighty big play for big stakes soon or else he's got woman trouble.' Stumpy stood up to clear the dishes away and clean up, leaving Stella to chew over his words.

Clint and Mex rode on under the increasing heat of the Colorado sun, the Texan totally unaware of the distress his manner had caused Stella. The two men chatted and smoked, completely ignoring the straight-backed figure of the bounty hunter trailing behind. Normally humane and generous, they had no time for a woman beater and no sympathy was wasted on Shand.

They arrived at the Lightning Flash a short while after Abe Ferris, the Sheriff of Brush County. Toft was sitting on the verandah in his company when Clint and Mex rode in with Shand. The rancher and his companion stood up and came down to ground level as Clint and Mex dismounted.

'Hiya, Bellamy,' said Toft. 'This is Abe Ferris, the Sheriff.'

Clint shook hands and introduced Mex to them. They grey haired Sheriff looked hard at Mex as he shook his hand.

'You from the Randall-Houston spread in Montana?' he asked and when Mex nodded: 'Mighty pleased to meet you, Mex. I've heard plenty about you from United States Marshal Wyatt.'

'Ha yes – Wyatt, mighty good lawman Wyatt,' replied Mex. 'Good tracker too. I reckon the States lost one good man when he settled down in Billings.'

Ferris nodded and looked at Shand without much enthusiasm.

'Why in heck have you got that bustard hogtied?' he asked.

Clint replied, giving the details briefly and both Ferris and Toft expressed their disgust with snorts of rage. A few punchers rolled up to view the bounty hunter and Toft addressed one of them.

'Cut that coyote down, Mog,' he said. 'See

that he gets a meal and hold him until Abe decides what to do with him.'

The puncher called Mog led Shand's saddle horse away and the other punchers followed behind. The bounty hunter remained silent.

'How's Barrett coming along?' Clint asked Toft as he followed with Mex into the big living room. The cattleman turned with a shrug.

'I guess he's feeling alright. Anyway, he rode out just after sun-up this morning. I guess he was afraid Abe would line up with Leverson.'

Clint and Mex exchanged glances.

'Did he say where he was heading?' Mex asked.

Toft shook his head. 'Nope. Just said he wanted to be free to hit back at whoever's trying to rub out the Rafter K. I reckon your guess is as good as mine.'

'Shand looks like he got mussed up in a stampede. You do that to him?' Ferris asked Clint, and when the youngster nodded, there was a look of respect in the lawman's bright blue eyes. 'It's my guess, Bellamy,' he added after a pause, 'We can let the bustard go now. You've given him punishment enough and he'll hightail it outa this territory plenty fast now that his reputation's tarnished. I'm gonna give him twenty-four hours to clear or he'll get shot on sight.'

Clint shrugged and grinned at the silver haired, whipcord tough oldster.

'You're the lawman and I reckon you know best.'

Ferris nodded. 'Yeah. I'll tell him I'm revokin' the reward on Barrett anyway. That'll leave him high and dry – puts him outside the law if he takes up the trail again.'

Toft motioned them to seats around the big redwood table and placed a bottle of bourbon and glasses in the middle. He poured out drinks and handed a box of cheroots round. Clint and Ferris declined the cheroots but Mex's eyes gleamed.

'Santos eh? Good brand,' he purred as he sniffed at the cheroot appreciatively. 'You're a man after my own heart, Toft.'

The rancher smiled at the Mexican's enthusiasm.

'Take yourself a handful if you like 'em, Mex,' he invited.

Mex did so without hesitation while Clint and Ferris rolled cigarettes.

'Well, Abe, we might as well bring you up to date with what's been happening on this range,' said Toft at length. 'Then if you'll give me your sayso, I'll get after that trail herd.'

Ferris took a long drink, refilled his glass and settled back in his chair. He remained silent while Toft told him about the rustlers who had driven off about three hundred head of his beeves after having knocked his night herder unconscious. He rifled through the bills of sale that Toft passed to him checking that all had been forged but making no comment.

After Toft had said his piece Mex told Ferris that Slim Murrow, the owner of the Straight Flush, and Mitchell's segundo had been amongst the rustlers.

'That don't prove Mitchell's tied up in things,' said Ferris quietly. 'I allow it looks mighty suspicious but Mitchell's put up a respectable front since hitting this range. Nope, it could be some of his hands are featherin' their nests.'

Neither Clint nor Mex went along with Ferris in that opinion but they were not prepared to push their own ideas. They were content to let the answers come.

Ferris pored over the bills again then finally pushed them over to Toft.

'Yeah, it sure looks as though this herd's been collected all along the trail the same way as they helped 'emselves to your stock. Guess I'll ride along with you. If it turns out the way we think then you get the all clear to take the herd over and I'll get the evidence to take in Murrow and Duke Lomas.'

'In that case I'll take Ben Holt's place an' he can look after the Lightning Flash.' Toft stood up with alacrity, eager to get things organised. Clint and Mex stood up as well.

'We'd sure like to be joining forces with

you, Toft,' said Clint. 'But we've got other chores. Hope you get all the breaks.'

Toft nodded his thanks.

'If you get hold of Barrett, keep him outa the way until I get back to Dallin,' put in Ferris. 'Then maybe we can set about clearing him of that killing charge.'

They shook hands and the pardners took their leave. When they rode out of the compound the place was alive with activity as the Lightning Flash hands prepared to do battle.

'Pretty tight outfit,' remarked Mex. 'Those drovers are in for a warm time.'

They took the Brush trail from the Lightning Flash. It took them up into the hills that formed the boundary between the Toft and Barrett spreads. Instead of dropping back down to the plain, they kept to the western rim of the hill. Far to the west, every now and again, the big sisters of the foothills showed out of the haze, the serried peaks of the vast Front Range rugged and impassable.

The foothills ran to the south and north, unbroken until at last the pardners arrived at Brush Gap. They dismounted at a point overlooking the gap where an overhang provided shelter from the fierce of the sun, and rustled themselves up a meal. While eating, they surveyed the terrain carefully but neither could see any reason why anyone would push for the Rafter K any more than for any other spread between Dallin and the Rockies.

'What do you make of it, Mex?' asked Clint at length as he rolled himself a cigarette and edged away from the Mexican's cheroot.

'Maybe the answer's under the ground. Could be somebody's stumbled on gold in these hills.'

Clint shook his head. 'Nope. I'd lay a dollar to every dime there's no gold this side of the Rockies 'cept maybe in Pike's Peak.'

Movement down below on the plain west of the gap brought the two men to their feet and they squinted down at the dots appearing and disappearing in the haze.

It was a long time before it was possible for them to pick out a rider leading a pack horse. At first they thought the rider was Shand but as the man closed the distance they could tell that he was of shorter, sturdier build. Now and again the man dismounted and gazed for a long time backtrail towards the north.

When he was about a mile away from the gap, the man dismounted and struggled to plant a stake in the ground. Then he did the same a couple more times before making the mouth of the gap. Reaching the gap, now just below the pardners, he spent some considerable time taking measurements and sighting from various points to where he had planted the stakes.

'Waal, I reckon we know the answer now, Clint,' said Mex as he eased back out of sight and lit another cheroot.

'Yeah, that hombre's got railroad written all over him. This gap must be the key to the whole business.' Clint struck one fist into the other in an unusual show of elation. 'Come on, Mex, let's go down an' palaver with him.'

They remounted and rode carefully down the steep sided hill, hitting the plain within hailing distance of the man. He watched them curiously as they rode up. The man was stockily built, of middle age, bronzed to the colour of teak, and the lines etched around his eyes spoke plainly of long hours squinting along grading posts and centre lines.

'Howdy,' said Clint and Mex in unison. The man grunted in reply.

'Railroad man eh?' Clint asked.

'What's it to you, Mister,' the man replied. 'I'm not asking you any questions.' He wore a gun slung low on his left side and looked as though he could use it. His whole de-meanour showed that he was spiky enough to court trouble rather than avoid it. Mex's eyes glittered nastily.

'You've got no call to be sassy, Mister.' His voice was smooth. 'There's been strange happenings on this range and a railroad through this pass could be the answer. If you're gonna be tight-lipped then I guess we can take it you're sided with the hombres stirring up the trouble.' He paused, a wicked smile flitting across his lips. 'We're set on salivating the trouble makers.'

The man looked unhurriedly from Mex to Clint. He was in no way perturbed and lit a cigarette with a steady hand.

'I don't know anything about trouble on this or any range,' he replied calmly. 'But I guess there's always trouble at the hint of a railroad. There's always someone trying to step in to make a fat profit.' He shrugged his shoulders. 'Me, I just happen to like my job. I work on my lonesome an' don't take sides with anyone.'

'If you don't take sides, Mister, how come somebody gets to know which way the rail-road's heading?' Clint's face was hard as he stared at the surveyor. The railroad man drew hard on his cigarette and his face tightened.

'I don't say which way the railroad goes. For most of the time I don't know. All I do is scout out the best and cheapest routes an' report 'em back to the planning office, then it's up to them.'

There was the stamp of independent honesty on the man's face and the hardness went out of Clint's features.

'Well, feller, I guess you're a straight shooter,' he remarked. 'But it sure looks as though somebody knows where the road's going down already.'

Mex eased out of the saddle to let his pinto

graze. He shared Clint's opinion that the man was straight as a rifle barrel and made his next question in a conversational tone.

'Who makes the decisions from the reports you send in?' The man shrugged the question away at first and stubbed the butt of his cigarette out on his boot; then squatted down on his heels.

'Well I can't see that any harm's done letting you know. I've surveyed three routes from Kansas City to Cheyenne and most of my reports have been in the planning office a long time. For the last few months I've just been double checking on points raised by the planning boss, Sam Mitchell, back at Kansas.'

Neither Clint nor Mex moved a face muscle as the name of the planning boss rolled off the man's tongue. 'Like I said,' the man continued. 'I still don't know for sure that the Company's gonna push on yet and if they do, they might go one of three ways.'

'I didn't get your moniker,' said Clint. 'I'm Bellamy and my pard's Mex Juarez.'

There wasn't a great deal of interest in the man's eyes. He was already thinking about some geographical hazard on the route he had just covered, but he nodded.

'I'm Wes Sutter, glad to know yuh.' He stood up. 'Now if that's all the palaverin' I'll collect my gear and head for Brush before nightfall.'

Mex got back into the saddle and the pards wheeled their horses round to go back through the gap. They gave the solitary man a wave as they left but he was too absorbed to return the farewell.

'Waal, the answer's as plain as a white faced maverick,' grinned Clint. 'Sam Mitchell gives the orders for the railroad to move on, and Steve Mitchell wants the Rafter K.' The grin faded as a significant thought crossed his mind. Time must be running short for Mitchell and they had left Stella under the protection of a one-armed man. A feeling of near panic rose up in him. Instinctively he knew that there was need for haste. He raised the horse's pace and Mex cast a quizzical eye after him before setting the pinto in pursuit.

CHAPTER ELEVEN

Steve Mitchell rode into Dallin early that day with his segundo, the deep chested Duke, and three other hard-looking punchers. Time was getting short. His brother wouldn't be able to keep the news back much longer and he'd have to tie things up mighty soon.

He was in the mood now to settle things and only waited long enough in Dallin to collect Marshal Leverson and Slim Murrow then they all headed out for the Rafter K. They were a grim bunch, urged on by thoughts of profit. Until now they had worked from under cover, putting on equable exteriors, but with Mitchell's intention to come into the open, the evil nature of the men bubbled to the surface and they were eager for action.

Luck was with them from the start. Slim Murrow, the restless deadly owner of the Straight Flush had ridden on ahead, impelled by some instinct. He caught a brief glimpse of Mal Barrett before the terrain swallowed the youngster up again. His keen eyes had recognised the Rafter K man immediately and with an evil grin he swung his horse around to rejoin the others. He reined in and held up his hand when the other riders rounded a bend. They hauled their cayuses to a stop.

'What's up?' growled Mitchell.

'We're gonna get company,' replied the suave Murrow. 'Mal Barrett's heading this way.'

Mitchell looked at him in surprise. With characteristic speed he grasped at the possibilities this bit of luck opened up and flashed a warning look around.

'Now, no gun play. I want Barrett alive and I want him to stay alive until he's served my purpose. Duke, take the boys ahead. Get under cover so you can take him from behind.'

The big segundo nodded and moved uptrail with the other two men to take up positions in the plentiful cover afforded by the huge boulders that lay in profusion beside the trail. Slim Murrow pulled his mount behind a boulder leaving Mitchell and Leverson holding the trail.

It was several minutes before Mal Barrett rounded the bend to come face to face with the waiting men. His hand dropped to his gun as he reined in and looked at them bitterly.

'Just keep away from your shooting irons, Leverson,' warned Mal. 'No two-bit crooked lawman's gonna take me in. You too, Mitchell,' he ground out. 'Your eyesight isn't too good anyway. If you couldn't see Faro go for his gun that night, then you're not gonna stack very high in a gun battle with me.'

'You must be loco, Mal,' grunted Mitchell. 'I guess Leverson's got a right to take you in but why should I go for my gun?'

Leverson looked completely disinterested. His heavy moustaches waggled as he spat a stream of tobacco juice at a lizard scurrying across the trail but Mitchell watched Mal closely. He was surprised at the change wrought in Barrett in such a short time. Deep grim lines were etched around his mouth and his eyes held nothing but menace. The rancher was mighty glad he had taken the precaution of planting his men in position to take care of the Rafter K man.

Leverson saw the glint of Murrow's gun and decided to push things. The sneer came off Mal's face as Leverson moved and his gun flashed out of its holster but it went spinning out of his hand as Murrow fired from cover. When he recovered from the surprise Mal found himself looking into Leverson's guns. Murrow came out into the open, smoke still curling lazily out of his gun muzzle. Duke and the other two men came up from behind and Mal realised with a sinking heart that his goose was cooked.

'Reckon I was right when I didn't trust you, Mitchell,' he remarked drily.

The rancher didn't answer Mal but addressed himself to Duke.

'You an' the boys take him back to the spread. Take good care of him. If he gives any trouble, take it out of his hide but I want him alive.'

Duke grinned and took Mal's other gun. He motioned to a surly red-headed man who took up the lead rein of Mal's horse then he and the other puncher fell in behind as Barrett was led away downtrail. Mitchell rubbed his hands in delight as they vanished from sight.

'Waal, I guess I've got plenty to bargain with now,' he chuckled. Leverson and

Murrow grinned with him and the three men gigged their mounts into a fast gallop towards the Rafter K.

It was a couple of hours after noon when they rode in on Stella and Hollister at the Brush Flats line shack. Seeing Mitchell, Stumpy didn't suspect any trouble and gave them a cheerful greeting, but Stella regarded the newcomers doubtfully.

'I'd like a few words with you, Stella,' said Mitchell. There was nothing in his manner to suggest that he was out to win her favours so she nodded. Murrow and Leverson moved in on Stumpy.

'How 'bout rustling up some chow,' growled the Marshal. 'I reckon I could eat the hind leg off'n a maverick.'

'Yeah, you set yourselves there an' I'll cook you something. Help yourselves to coffee,' grinned Stumpy.

Leverson and Murrow helped themselves to a mug of coffee apiece and picked the shady side of the line shack where they sat back on their heels to wait for the meal and for Mitchell to get his business done. The rancher moved out of earshot with Stella and leaned carelessly against the loaded chuck wagon. Grim-faced and overbearing, he looked straight at Stella.

'You'd better get your things together, Stella,' he said briefly. 'You're due to marry me pronto.'

A quick reply flashed into the girl's mind but the cold look in Mitchell's eyes made her think again.

'You don't seriously expect me to marry you just like that, Steve,' she faltered, and when Mitchell merely shrugged, 'What makes it so important to you?'

'If you want to keep Mal alive, you'd better do like I said and get your things together.'

The girl looked her surprise – this was a new Mitchell. Gone were the cheery smile and disarming manner. He looked brash, hard and dominating.

'What do you know about Mal?' she asked as fears started to crowd in on her.

'Plenty,' he retorted. 'Right now I've got him over in my spread. If you play things right and marry me straight away he'll be safe where he is but if you've got other ideas then I'll turn him out an' he'll get shot on sight for the reward. Plenty of my boys are ready to pick up easy money.'

'What is it you want? Surely marrying me isn't worth the blood of my brother on your hands?'

'You'll do as I say or plenty of blood's gonna be spilled. Mal's for a start an' that blamed Bellamy's next.'

Stella was silent for a long time. Things had taken a turn she couldn't understand. She had thought Mal was safe at the Lightning Flash and now Mitchell stated he was at the

180

Lone Star. If only Clint and his pardner were on hand to sort things out. She bit her lip as the thought of Clint's blood being spilled assumed greater disaster in her mind to that of Mal's.

'I'll not do as you say until I've seen Mal and know that he's alright,' she said at length.

Mitchell nodded. 'I guess that's fair enough. Slim can ride in for that two-bit preacher an' bring him into the Lone Star right away.'

Stella shook her head and the determination in her face matched his. 'No, Steve, I'll come with you to check on Mal and on your promise that he'll come to no harm, I'll go into Dallin and get myself a dress suited to a wedding. We can get married in three days and no less. You can take that or leave it.'

Mitchell mulled over things in his mind. He still had a little time left to play with before the news of the railroad's next move broke, and three days wouldn't make much difference. Come to think of it, he'd be wise to concede something to her. If he sweetened the terms a bit then she might give freely in marriage what he was prepared to take by force. He allowed his features to relax a little and something of the old charm broke through.

'Yeah. I guess a woman must have things just right for a wedding. Three days it'll be. But you just tell Stumpy loud and clear before we ride out that you're marrying me so he can pass the news on to that pair of saddle tramps Bellamy and Juarez.'

Stella gave a quick nod of acquiescence and went inside the line shack to collect some of her clothing together. Mitchell strolled over to the fire and helped himself to a mug of coffee. He was well satisfied. On their wedding day Mal Barrett would die, shot while trying to escape from the custody of one of Mitchell's men. That would leave Mitchell in control of his wife's interest in the Rafter K.

For her part Stella prayed that Clint and Mex would somehow intervene and save her from the desperate situation in which her concern for Mal had placed her, but why they should, and how, were two points that eluded her.

When she came back outside with her leather travelling satchel, Mitchell was eating the meal Stumpy had prepared, in company with Leverson and Murrow. Leverson ignored her but Murrow let his glance steal over her in a sensual way that made her flush angrily. Mitchell intercepted the look and merely laughed. Stumpy offered her some coffee but she refused it and went over to where her horse grazed. She led the animal back to the chuck wagon and saddled up. When she was ready, she waited for the others to finish their meal. Hollister looked uncertainly towards Stella and scratched his head in a perplexed sort of way as he tried to figure out why she should be riding out now against Bellamy's instructions.

'Waal, I guess we'd better be riding,' said Mitchell at length, tossing his empty plate to Stumpy. 'Miss Stella's coming with us. She'll tell you why.'

Leverson and Murrow stood up and followed to where their horses grazed. They all mounted and Stella climbed into the saddle. She rode up to Hollister and when she spoke to him, her expression hardly conveyed the right amount of enthusiasm to match the import of her words.

'I'm riding in to the Lone Star and then into Dallin. I'm marrying Steve Mitchell in a couple of days. You'd better hang on here until we make plans for all this stuff.'

'Yeah, that's right. You do like Miss Stella says,' boomed Mitchell.

Hollister nodded dumbly, his gaze fixed on the moisture that gathered and hung on Stella's lower lashes. In that moment he knew something was up. Some of the old fire smouldered up in the one-armed man.

'An' you see you take durned care of her, Mitchell,' he snarled. 'Or I'll have your hide for buzzards meat.'

The look Mitchell flashed Stumpy before the riders moved off had none of the old Mitchell in it and Hollister shivered involuntarily as the full venom of the man's nature

183

became apparent to him for the first time. He sat down near the fire under the full blast of the scorching sun, scarcely noticing the discomfort as he tried to sort things out in his mind.

It was a long time before Stumpy stirred himself to collect more fuel for the fire and to make another brew of coffee. He waited with growing impatience for Clint and Mex to return.

When eventually the two pardners rode in, the solemn expression on Stumpy's face told them immediately that something was amiss. Clint looked around the shack quickly for sign of Stella and groaned aloud when he saw that her horse was gone.

'Where's Stella?' he shouted. Mex was studying the ground, his quick eyes picking up enough evidence to fill three quarters of the story.

'She's gone with Steve Mitchell, Leverson and Murrow,' Stumpy replied. 'Told me she was goin' into Dallin after the Lone Star, an' that she'd be gettin' wed to Mitchell in a coupla days.'

Clint could only stare at the little man bleakly. The words reverberated around inside his mind like the knell of doom. All of a sudden he felt a heaviness within that seemed to spread until he felt his chest would burst. With an effort he pulled himself together and slid out of the saddle, leaving the horse to make its own way to the nearby stream. He reached for a mug of coffee and sipped the scalding liquid without noticing the pain while he stared unseeingly into the fire.

Mex dismounted and led his horse to the stream where he controlled the intake of both the pinto and dun gelding. He had known that Clint had taken a strong fancy to Stella but only now did he realise just how much the Texan cared for her. The Mexican's face was serious for although always ready to make light of infatuations, he respected real love and gave it its full value. If Clint felt that way then he'd make it his business to negotiate the most satisfactory ending.

After removing the saddles and bridles from their horses, Mex strolled over to the fire and helped himself to coffee. Clint looked up after a while, his face strained and tense.

'Guess there's nothing left for us to do here, Mex,' he said. 'Seems that Miss Stella thinks sharing things with Mitchell is a good idea. With Mitchell taking over that lets us out.'

The Mexican fixed him with his bright eyes and shook his head.

'Nope, Clint. I reckon you're not seeing things straight. It's my bet that Mitchell had found something else to twist her arm with.'

'What do you mean?' broke in Hollister. 'What is it you know about Mitchell?'

185

Mex told him about the possibility of the railroad pushing through Rafter K territory and the coincidence of the railroad official being one Sam Mitchell. As he spoke the light of understanding grew brighter in Stumpy's eyes.

'Goldarn it! That sure explains why Miss Stella was near to crying when she told me she was marrying Mitchell,' he roared. 'I just couldn't understand it. Why, the dirty slit-eyed coyote, he must have been threatenin' her while Leverson and Murrow kept me busy. I'll salivate that hombre for sure!'

The weight lifted from Clint's chest and he grabbed Stumpy as the oldster went to dash for his saddle.

'Take it easy. You said in a couple of days they were going to get wed? Well, you just get busy rustling up something to eat. Whatever we're going to do will be done after a lot of thought.'

Mex nodded his approval and smiled as he saw the strained lines ease out of the youngster's face.

'Y'know, Clint,' he began as he searched in his pockets for a cheroot. 'We know where Miss Stella's gone an' where she'll be so there's no call to go riding into the Lone Star. It's my guess we'll do better to back-track Mitchell the way he came. Could be we'll find how he was able to put the squeeze on Stella.'

'Yeah, I'd got to thinking that myself.' Clint's spirits had risen to such a degree that he forgot to snort with disgust and move out of range as Mex lit the cheroot.

Hollister looked up at the pards from the pan that he was warming through.

'I'm coming this time, you fellers,' he announced. 'Durned if I'm gonna whittle my time away herding a load of junk while I can tote a gun.'

'It's up to you I guess,' said Clint. 'I reckon you feel pretty well burned up.'

Mex took a look at the position of the setting sun and sat down.

'Not much good back-tracking this late. There'll be no moon for a couple of hours after nightfall,' he said. 'We'll get some shut-eye an' start out at sun-up.'

Wilt Shand hauled his mount around and took the trail that led back over the hills to Rafter K territory. His mind had started to see things clearly again after being filled with black brooding from the beating he had taken. He reined in, dismounted and going to the pack horse, rummaged in one of the packs, bringing out a long barrelled colt and a fresh gunbelt. He fastened on the belt and slipped the gun into its holster.

When Abe Ferris had told him to clear out of the territory, he had set his horse to the west unthinking, instinct making him strike

north to the other side of the hills for Cheyenne and west again to Idaho where his
name stacked high, but with each mile the
fact became clearer that he could never be
anything again whilst Bellamy lived. It
mattered not one bit how he effected the
Texan's death. As long as he was responsible
for it, then he would be able to resume his
grisly profession.

Remounting, he travelled inexorably towards the line shack, his mind a cauldron of
hate. He was stretched full length behind a
sheltering shrub, looking down at the line
shack, when the sun edged up over the
prairie line and the three men below rode
away towards Dallin. He allowed them to
get well clear before riding down and cooking himself a meal from their provisions.

He told himself there was no need for
hurry. Bellamy and his pards had ridden out
as though they had a set mission so they
should be away for some time. Searching
around, he found his Sharps rifle, his own
well tried Colts and plenty of ammunition
for the rifle. With the rifle back in his saddle
holster and his favourite guns strapped
down tightly to his thighs, the confidence
started to creep back into his mind. Even
now Shand ached in every limb from the
hammering Clint had given him but his
pride had suffered worse. Although he
would not admit so to himself he was al-

ready set to kill the Texan from ambush.

It didn't strike Shand that he was lucky to be alive and free. For ill-using a woman the way he had, Clint could have shot him in cold blood after the beating and been completely exonerated, or else Ferris could have held him in chokey for a long time. Ferris's parting threat came back to him as he mounted his horse.

'If I catch you in this territory after sun-up I'll shoot you down like the vermin you are!'

Shand shrugged and set his cayuse towards the hills, the pack horse following behind on the end of its lead rein. He wouldn't stay long enough in this territory after Bellamy's death for anyone to catch up with him and there was no one more able to hide himself away than Shand.

Some distance up in the hills, he dismounted and unloaded the pack horse. He took out certain items from the packs, rolling them up in his saddle roll then hiding the packs behind a boulder: he set the horse free and climbing into the saddle rode back down to the line shack and picked up Bellamy's trail.

CHAPTER TWELVE

Clint, Mex and Hollister had no difficulty in back-tracking Mitchell and his companions to the point where Mal had met up with them. Mex dismounted here and spent a long time searching around the trail. Clint sat in the saddle, smoking. He was well able to read sign but he knew Mex was the equal of any scout the west had produced. After a few minutes Mex remounted and rode off uptrail to where Murrow stopped when he had caught the first glimpse of Mal. The Mexican spotted where a rider had come downtrail then the picture of events was clear to him. He returned to where the others waited. Clint looked at him questioningly.

'It's my guess that when Mal Barrett got fed up with nursing his wounds and left Toft's spread, he headed this way. Anyway a rider whoever he was met up with Mitchell and his crew right here. Most of the crew were hiding off the trail when he came up. Mitchell, Leverson and Murrow came on to the line shack. The other three riders and the one I take to be Mal went downtrail.'

'Bet you're right at that, Mex,' Clint answered. 'It must have been Mal. That's why

Mitchell was able to put the squeeze on Stella.'

'Waal, let's get after the bastards,' growled Hollister.

Mex and Clint exchanged glances. The little oldster would have to be held in check or his impetuosity would give them trouble.

'Look, Stumpy,' Clint said patiently. 'We're not just gonna horn in on things with six-guns blazing. That way we'll all end up dead an' Mitchell will get what he's after. You keep hold of your temper an' we'll do things in our own way.'

'Shucks, Clint. I may be a bit hot under the collar but I'll play it your way. I wouldn't want to do anything that would go against Miss Stella's chances of gettin' clear out of trouble.'

Clint grinned and leaned over to pat the oldster on the shoulders.

'Come on then. Let's see where they took Mal.'

They followed the trail easily enough to where the riders had struck off over the foothills towards the Lone Star ranch. They carried on through the foothills and holed up overlooking the lush pastures of Mitchell's Lone Star. Down below cattle grazed and now and again a rider circled the animals then headed west towards another group of cattle just visible through the haze.

With infinite patience they waited while the

191

sun blazed its way across the sky and finally dropped beyond the distant mountains. As the stars gathered strength in the cloudless heavens they made ready to invade Lone Star territory. Clint voiced the thought that had been with him for some time.

'I reckon two of us can handle this end of things, Stumpy,' he remarked. 'It could be you'd be more help keeping your eyes open in town. If Stella is gonna be in Dallin you can watch out for her an' keep an eye on anything connected with Mitchell, Murrow an' that so-called lawman.'

Mex nodded his agreement but Stumpy thought long and hard before agreeing. The little oldster had a yen to be in the middle of things.

'If that's the way you want it, I'll head in muy pronto,' he said at length.

'That sure sets my mind at rest.' There was sincerity in Clint's voice and Stumpy felt gratified. 'If anyone asks why you left the line shack just tell 'em that you figured you had a right to be on hand when your boss got married. I guess that's sense enough for anyone. But don't even tell Stella that we're set on springing Mal. Any change in her manner could warn Mitchell.'

'Yeah, you leave it to me. I'll keep mighty close to anything that's goin' on.' Determined lines settled on Stumpy's face. 'Just in case you fellers meet up with trouble, I'm telling you now that Mitchell's not going to get hitched with Miss Stella. If you haven't shown up by the time the wedding's due, I'll ventilate him for sure.'

'I reckon you'll save her a lot of grief if you do just that,' said Mex. 'But I sure hope you won't be left with that chore.'

Stumpy hauled his cayuse round to cut through the hills back on to the Dallin trail and the two pardners waved a farewell as they set their mounts downgrade.

They rode at an easy pace, maintaining almost complete silence. During their vigil in the hills they had oiled all leather work so that no part of their equipment creaked, and everything that might have jingled was fastened down. The first bunch of cattle they skirted were still grazing half-heartedly but groups they picked later had settled down for the night. A couple of times they froze into immobility as the creaking of leather and jingling of spurs heralded the approach of a rider but each time the rider passed on without noticing them. They were prepared to deal with any Lone Star man who wandered into their path but preferred to avoid using firearms if possible so as not to start a stampede. Any large scale movement on the part of dozing cattle would alert too many hands.

With the gathering chorus of the cicadas for accompaniment they continued through the night until they reached the circle of cottonwoods that sheltered the Lone Star headquarters. There they dismounted, leaving their horses picketed within the cover of the shadowy mass of trees.

On the fringe of the cottonwoods they stared down at the ranch compound for a long time, getting the feel of the place by listening intently for sounds of movement. Light gleamed beyond the verandah of the ranch-house from windows set each side of the door. This opened once for a man to leave for what must have been the bunk-house. A few seconds later another door opened and a shaft of light widened, was lost for a moment as a man went through, then narrowed and vanished as the door shut.

The pards were in no hurry. Better to let the ranch-house settle down for the night before getting down amongst things. They whiled away the time, speaking together in whispers. They had been in position for about an hour when a couple of riders came in. For another half an hour or so the riders could be traced around the compound by the noise they made, first seeing to their mounts, then getting themselves something to eat from the dining hall. Finally the bunkhouse door opened and shut and a pall of silence spread again, broken only by the distant howl of coyotes and the never ceasing background of the cicadas.

One of the windows in the ranch-house blacked out as the light in one room was extinguished then the door opened and two figures were silhouetted on the verandah until the door closed again. The pards listened intently in an attempt to pick up the men's movements but until a couple of lights flared up in the vicinity of the verandah they could not trace the position of the men. Obviously these had been deputed as guards outside the house and now they were treating their duty lightly, smoking quite openly.

'We've got about two hours before the moon comes up, Clint,' whispered Mex. 'If we sweat it out another hour I reckon those two hombres'll be asleep.'

'I sure hope you're right,' agreed Clint. 'Why in the heck have they gotta smoke? It sets up a hankering, watching them cigarettes burn.'

Mex mumbled his agreement but drew some solace from chewing at the end of one of his cheroots.

The cigarettes went out at last and they heard the guards stamp around the building once then settle down on the verandah. The minutes dragged away until the hour had passed.

'Righto, Mex, now's the time,' said Clint. 'I'll take the one on the left.'

They moved like wraiths away from the cottonwoods and down amongst the ranch buildings. A horse nickered and they froze in the deeper shadows of the dining hall but no one was alerted and they edged cautiously towards the ranch-house.

Gaining the end of the building they stooped low and inched along at the foot of the verandah. Coming to the steps they paused and carefully probed the shadows until they made out the nodding figures of the sentries. Cautiously they eased out their six-guns and grasping the barrels, soft-footed on to the first step. It creaked loudly and one of the guards stirred. His movement galvanised the pardners into action; together they made the verandah at a rush. Their gun butts cracked down on to the guards' heads simultaneously and one of them gave out a low groan. Then there was silence as the pards held on to the men, allowing them to slide gently to the floor on the verandah.

The next part tested the nerves of both men. Clint waited on the verandah, ready to act should anyone emerge from the house, whilst Mex made his way to the big stable at the end of the corral to saddle up a mount should their surmise be correct and Barrett prove to be a prisoner inside the ranch-house.

It took Mex about a quarter of an hour to saddle up an animal in the dark and muffle the horse's hooves with sacking but after what had seemed an age to Clint, he was back and the animal was hitched to the verandah rail.

Clint squeezed the Mexican's arm as if to say 'This is it!' then tried the door. It gave easily and without noise. One after the other they slid inside the house, closing the door gently behind them. They were in a big room and a thin line of light showed under a door leading off to the right.

For a long time they stayed in one place hardly daring to breathe while their eyes became accustomed to the deeper gloom of the house, but at length they were able to pick out the darker blur of objects and pinpoint them as chairs, settle, table and cabinet.

Mex eased up to the door where the light showed underneath and listened intently. Clint joined him. The door must have been mighty thick because it was only by placing their ears against the wood that the muffled voices reached them.

'Card game goin' on,' whispered Mex. 'Mebbe they've got Mal in another room.'

'Yeah but I guess we'll do better by busting in,' replied Clint softly. 'Ready?'

'Yeah,' breathed Mex and Clint took hold of the door knob carefully. It turned smoothly then when the catch was completely free he threw the door open and stepped inside the room with Mex at his shoulder.

Three men were huddled around a card

table. One empty bottle and another half full of rye stood on it and in front of each man was a half-filled glass. In a corner on a palliasse lay Mal Barrett, bound hand and foot, but asleep.

'Freeze!' ordered Clint.

The two men facing him looked in blank amazement at the pards and the guns pointing menacingly in their direction. The third man turned his head slowly, his expression totally disbelieving. Barrett woke up and at first regarded them woodenly, then a big grin spread over his face.

'Am I glad to see you fellers,' he said.

Mex holstered one of his guns and taking out his knife, stepped around Clint to cut Barrett's bonds. The three punchers had consumed enough rye that night, however, to make them reckless and one went for his gun. Before it had cleared leather the knife was embedded to the hilt in his chest. With uncanny skill, Mex had spun the knife with deadly accuracy and the man sagged and clawed with one hand at the table whilst the other came up from his gun to the knife handle. He died before he hit the ground.

The other two men froze as instructed and Mex stepped over to the corpse, extracted the knife, wiped it casually on the dead man's clothes and cut Barrett free. Mal sat up and rubbed at his wrists in turn.

'There's a bronc outside, Barrett,' said

Mex. 'When you leave, go straight around the left hand side o' this place and head up to the cottonwoods at the top of the rise. Wait for us there.'

Mal stood up and staggered a little as he waited for the circulation to come back in his feet.

'I guess I'm always having to thank you two hombres,' he said. 'Mebbe some day I'll do you a turn.'

'Mind you do when you get the chance,' grinned Clint.

Mal moved to where the dead man lay and unclasping the gunbelt, dragged it from underneath the body and made to buckle it on. As Mex moved to disarm the other two men, the one facing Clint, a big burly man, went for his gun. The other followed suit, jumping sideways and clawing for his gun on the turn.

Both punchers were fast, deadly gunmen but facing Clint with his guns ready, they were doomed from the word go. A split second after his six-guns barked they slumped to join their former comrade on the floor.

'Get moving, Barrett!' shouted Clint. 'We'll cover in case anyone else takes a hand.'

Mal needed no further bidding and headed out of the room for the outer door. One of the guards had recovered and stood framed in the doorway. Mex shot him as he brought his gun to bear and Mal jumped over the man's fallen body.

As Mal unhitched the horse and swung into the saddle, stabs of flame flashed from the direction of the bunkhouse. The horse squealed as a bullet seared its hindquarters and Barrett had a job gaining control before the animal set off at speed for the cotton-woods. More bullets thudded into the verandah close to the pardners but they held their fire.

As Barrett's horse sped out of the com-pound, the pardners heard the men from the bunkhouse race to a point where noth-ing impeded their aim. As the men's guns flashed, sending bullets in the direction of the escaping rider, Clint and Mex opened up at the tell-tale flashes.

There was one low moan, and another curse as a man fell and a gun went clattering to the ground. They heard someone scurry back to the safety of the bunkhouse. The door slammed and they heard the bolt rammed home.

'Come on!' said Clint, his nerves all a-tingle with excitement. 'Looks like most of Mitchell's hands are in Dallin.'

The moon edged up as he spoke, a little ahead of their predictions, shedding a thin light over the scene, and they scudded around the side of the ranch-house then scrambled up the slope towards the cotton-woods.

When halfway up they heard two shots and a scream from above and their spirits sank as they feared the night's work had been in vain.

Wilt Shand stuck doggedly to the trail left by the Rafter K men, his mind obsessed by the dark desperate need to kill Bellamy. He chewed at his plug tobacco mechanically, scarcely noticing when some of the juice ran its searing course down to his stomach. The red blood mist was in his mind and he had no thought other than the fate the Texan should suffer. He would have liked to take Bellamy alive and somewhere up in the hills, stake him out and let the blood drain slowly out of him, to see him die by inches, but he knew that death would have to be sudden or else Bellamy would be a danger to him up to the last drop.

Skilled to the utmost degree as a tracker, he kept just the right distance between him and his quarry. By instinct he knew they had no intention of striking Lone Star territory by day, and making a wide detour came into position well above where the Rafter K men holed up, and from where he was able to lie full length and watch them.

The range was too great for complete accuracy with the rifle and he considered the terrain carefully with a view to getting nearer. He gave up the thought at last. There was no way of getting closer to the men without taking a chance on being seen and he doubted that much moved without being seen within the orbit of Bellamy and Juarez.

Just before nightfall he saw the preparations being made to ride and with the last glimmer of daylight saw Hollister head back the way they had come, the other two riding down on to Lone Star pasture. Walking back to where he had ground-hitched his horse, he mounted and set off in pursuit of the pards.

After years of night tracking nature had equipped him with a sort of built-in capacity to follow a scent in the manner of a homing pigeon seeking its loft. His eyes, accustomed to the dark, picked up deeper banks of blackness caused by solid objects at long range and unerringly he followed the unsuspecting pardners. Never did he get near enough to give them warning.

By the time Clint and Mex reached the cottonwoods, Shand knew for sure that they would be making an attempt to gain entry to the Lone Star under cover of darkness. He was in no way curious as to the reason. All that mattered to him was that when eventually the pards made their getaway, they might do so at speed and in near panic. That would be the time to kill the pair of them. He licked his lips in anticipation like a vampire.

Leaving his horse outside the ring of cottonwoods on the north side and with practiced skill, he edged his way through the shrubs and thickets that abounded in the shadow of the taller trees. After a long patient foray, he came to where the acrid smell of horse sweat filled the light breeze, and then froze for a long time.

It was much later that he was sure Bellamy and the Mexican had moved on away from where their horses stood and only then did Wilt Shand move in close. He played around for a while with the thought of unfastening the cinches so that when the pards tried to mount they would slide off with their saddles but he dismissed the idea because whereas it would give him an advantage over the nearest to his gun, the other man would temporarily be under the cover of the foremost horse. He took up a position behind a tree, a few feet from where the horses stood nodding, and settled down to wait.

Time passed interminably but Shand had waited through many a night under similar circumstances and always the high excitement of a killing in prospect had fortified him. He had reached the point of slavering in ghoulish anticipation when two shots ripped away the night's silence.

There was a brief pause then another shot and Shand cursed in his fear that he might be deprived of his victim.

More shots rang out and as the moon broke into the heavens, Shand, now drunk with his desire to kill, ran madly to the edge of the cottonwoods. The moonlight picked out his gaunt frame as Mal Barrett rode his maddened mount up the slope.

Mal saw Shand's gun come up and clawed for his own weapon. A spurt of flame burst as the bounty hunter fired and the horse stopped running, seeming to die in mid-air. Barrett leapt clear, crashing to the ground and rolled half a dozen times before firing. An awful scream rang out from Shand as the bullet from Mal's gun went into his spleen and he hovered a long time like a smaller less durable sort of cottonwood before pitching head first to lie beside the horse's twitching body.

A couple of minutes later Clint and Mex came panting up to the crest. Mal was picking himself up painfully. His fall had started up the throbbing in his head again.

'You alright, Barrett?' Mex called as they came abreast.

'Yeah. I think I got the bastard,' Mal answered.

Clint was looking down at the long skinny form, lying in a rapidly growing pool of blood.

'Wilt Shand!' he exclaimed.

'Who?' asked Mex.

'Shand,' Clint said again. 'I reckon that's justice. He must have left his cayuse around somewhere. You'd better take his, Barrett.'

Mex hauled Mal to his feet and stayed with him while Clint collected the two horses and then mounting the gelding rode round the cottonwoods to look for Shand's horse. In a few minutes the Texan returned leading the spare cayuse.

'We'll take Shand's body along,' said Mex. 'It'll give us a bit of an edge when we hit town. Folk in Dallin seemed to think he was the last word in gunslingers. Might stop a few getting itchy fingers in case they get the same medicine.'

'Can't say I cared much for his company before Mal plugged him,' said Clint sourly. 'But I reckon you're right, Mex. Give me a hand to get him up in front of my saddle.'

Whoever was left in the bunkhouse of the Lone Star, must have had a healthy regard for his safety, for he remained under cover during all the time it took the three men to tie Shand's body across the front of Clint's saddle pommel and ride away well clear of the Lone Star headquarters.

As the Rafter K men circled the ranch buildings and headed for Dallin, Clint and Mex filled in all the details for Mal Barrett.

'Y'know, Mal,' said Clint at length. 'It looks as though you wiped the slate clean for anything me an' Mex might've done. Shand was waiting to wipe us out for sure and if the shooting hadn't pulled him out of hiding, he might have been lucky.'

'If you fellers can call it square, I'm mighty obliged,' replied Mal with a cheerfulness that had been missing for a long time. 'By my reckoning I'm way behind.'

'Plenty of chores left yet,' put in Mex. 'Ain't no time to start in congratulating each other.'

The others laughed and feeling in high spirits lit up cigarettes. Mex dug out a cheroot and moved upwind of them just to savour Clint's remarks.

CHAPTER THIRTEEN

Stumpy Hollister rode into Dallin just before midnight. He stabled his horse in the livery stable and made his way to the Straight Flush saloon. His throat felt as though it was lined with sandpaper and his pace increased as he drew nearer to the saloon. He would have preferred to use the Frontiersman which was run by an old pard of his but it was his job to keep tabs on Mitchell and the Lone Star boss always used the Straight Flush.

The saloon was filled and noisy and the smoke lay thick and low, nearly blotting out the light from the lamps that hung from the cross beams but Stumpy pushed his way to the bar without acknowledging anyone.

Finding a blank space he squeezed in and tossed a coin on the counter. The barkeep came up and automatically reached for the bourbon that Stumpy favoured.

'Ain't seen you around for a long time, Hollister,' the barkeep said. 'Thought you'd turned pussyfoot.'

Stumpy gave him a sour look and poured himself a liberal drink which he downed in one. He treated the second drink the same way then with a third in front of him, took stock of the crowded saloon.

For the most part the same men occupied the same tables they had occupied when he was last in the saloon and the dance hostesses were the same pallid lack-lustre crew he'd ignored many times in the past. As he cast his eye up the bar he caught sight of Mitchell just as the rancher edged away from the bar and looked in his direction. Mitchell's face hardened and he pushed his way down to where Hollister stood.

'Thought I told you to stay put out at the line shack, Hollister,' he growled.

Stumpy took a long drink then glared up at the Lone Star man.

'Since when have I taken your orders?' he answered. 'It was alright for Miss Stella to tell me but I got to thinking – if you an' her are gonna get hitched, that makes you running the Rafter K. Well, I just quit.'

Mitchell's face purpled and it was with

considerable difficulty that he mastered his feelings.

'Well, I guess you're free to quit,' he said. 'But don't come around looking for hand-outs when the dinero runs out.'

'What in heck's got into you, Mitchell?' asked Hollister, surprise patent on his wrinkled face. 'If I were a young feller getting hitched to a gal like Stella Barrett, I'd be a mite more cheerful.'

Mitchell went to make a reply then thought better of it. He turned away with a shrug and rejoined Murrow who leaned casually against his own bar. Stumpy appeared to turn his full attention on his drink but he kept darting glances in the long mirror, keeping the two men under surveillance.

A few minutes later Murrow pushed next to the little oldster. He motioned up to the barkeep.

'Set up another bottle of that on the house,' he said quietly.

'Sure thing, Mister Murrow,' the barkeep answered and placed another full bottle beside the one Stumpy was punishing.

'Have that one on me, Stumpy. Can't blame you comin' in for a bit o' life.' The saloon keeper smiled but Hollister noticed that his eyes didn't keep pace with his lips. Stumpy wasn't worried. He might as well drink Murrow's bourbon as anyone else's. 'Mitchell tells me you've quit the Rafter K because your boss is gettin' herself hitched up to him.' Stumpy nodded. 'I guess you've allus been a hundred per cent worker an' if you need a job I reckon I can fit you in.'

Hollister looked at him in some surprise but took a pull at his drink before answering.

'That's mighty good of you, Slim,' he said. 'But I don't aim to hang around town. I guess I'll get by.'

'Waal, it's up to you. If you change your mind let me know.' Murrow turned to go away then as if an afterthought had struck him swivelled round again.

'Those other two saddle tramps, Bellamy and Juarez – did they quit too?'

Stumpy grinned to himself. This was the reason for the bourbon and offer of a job.

'Yeah, they quit,' he answered. 'I reckon it was seeing them quit that put the idea in my mind. They didn't think they'd get along with Mitchell.'

'Which way did they head?' Murrow made it sound casual.

'Through the hills, south for Colorado Springs. Said they intended going clear through New Mexico to Texas.' Stumpy shook his head sorrowfully. 'I was mighty sorry to see 'em go. Regular fire-eaters those hombres. They sure handled them fire-raising Vigilantes.'

That was a subject Murrow preferred to leave alone and with a grin he patted Stumpy on the back and returned to where Mitchell talked to Leverson who had just entered the saloon. Murrow spoke a few words to them and Hollister saw the expression of relief flood across Mitchell's face. He grinned into his drink and started in on Murrow's bourbon.

As customers moved around, he edged further up the bar until he was quite close to the three men, but he heard nothing of any interest until a dust covered cowpoke entered the saloon and after a quick look round made his way to where Mitchell, Murrow and Leverson talked. Mitchell's face was grim as he surveyed the man but the newcomer was a hefty, hard-looker who pushed between the three men casually to get to the bar.

'What the heck are you doing here, Rimmer?' asked Mitchell in loud enough tones to reach Stumpy.

'Come to collect a few bucks from you fellers before movin' on,' Rimmer replied easily. 'That trail herd – you ain't runnin' it any longer.'

Stumpy edged still closer. He saw Murrow's eyes narrow and a nerve start to twitch high in the temple. The saloon keeper was getting annoyed.

'Say what you mean, Rimmer,' he snarled.

The man shrugged and downed a drink he had poured for himself.

'We got jumped. Half the boys took tickets

for Boot Hill an' a few more are holed up nursin' chunks of lead. It looks like we started something when we run off with Lightning Flash beef. Anyways that trail herd's on its way to Kansas City an' the Lightning Flash crew's herdin' it.'

Murrow took in a deep breath and turned to Mitchell.

'Your boys are in town, Steve. I reckon we'd better move in and take that herd back. I don't aim to let anyone muscle in on my share.'

Mitchell shook his head.

'Nope, my boys stay put until I've settled things here. Take it easy a couple of days and we'll horn in on Toft's outfit. No harm in 'em taking over the chores for a bit. It'll leave us less ground to cover to Kansas.'

'You're gonna have a mighty tough job takin' that herd back,' said Rimmer. 'That Toft runs a spunky outfit.' He took another pull from his glass before continuing. 'They've got the law on their side too. Regular two-gun humdinger called Ferris, so Curley Noyes said just before he took his ticket for Boot Hill.' Rimmer looked at Leverson with amusement as he added the last bit. The apprehension that showed briefly in the Marshal's eyes seemed to give the trail drover some satisfaction.

The news that Abe Ferris had taken a hand in things seemed to shake all three men until Murrow faced up to the situation with a shrug.

'Waal, I guess we'll just have to liquidate old Abe and run Leverson for Sheriff. You gonna take a hand, Rimmer, when we ride?'

The driver shrugged indifferently.

'Luke Mappin's dead as you well know,' he replied. 'Cut me in on to his share an' trail boss pay, an' I'll ride.'

The three men flashed glances at each other and Mitchell nodded shortly. He pulled out a roll of bills and detaching some, handed them to the drover.

'That'll take care of you for a bit,' he growled. 'See us tomorrow and we'll tie up your cut.'

Rimmer pocketed the bills, ordered himself a bottle and crossed to a table. Within a couple of minutes he was joined by a loose-limbed hostess and was well set towards enjoying himself.

Stumpy edged away. He had heard enough and for another hour or so gave himself up to the enjoyment of drinking. He was nicely mellowed when at last he made his unsteady way to a bed at the Frontiersman.

It was just thirty minutes before sun-up when Clint, Mex and Mal Barrett reined in with Dallin just a quarter of a mile away. They checked their guns methodically then looked at each other with set expressions.

'There's stabling at the back of the Frontiersman. That's the second on the left down Main Street,' said Barrett. 'Stumpy'll be there for sure. His pard Levi Rudge owns the place. Old Sangster, the potman, will be awake now. He'll get us up to Stumpy without anyone knowing.'

'That's just dandy,' said Clint. 'Let's muffle these broncs. No point in waking up the town before we're ready.'

'I reckon the best place to leave the corpse is in front of the Marshal's office,' said Mex with a grin. 'Should cause quite a stir.'

They fixed pads on to the horses' hooves and after transferring the dead bounty hunter on to his own cayuse, rode into town.

As Mal had said, Sangster, the wizened old potman of the Frontiersman, was up and doing. Barrett and Clint slid through the open door into his kitchen while Mex walked Shand's horse round to the hitchrail in front of the Marshal's office.

The sudden appearance of two men in his kitchen failed to disturb Sangster. In a long eventful life he had seen it all and took things as they came. His sharp eyes scrutinised them carefully.

'Glad to know you stopped runnin', Barrett,' he said briefly.

Clint was pleased to see that Mal didn't take offence at the old man's remarks. Barrett had really grown up of late.

'Yeah, I ain't got the wind for it,' replied Mal with a smile. 'Did Hollister come in during the night?'

'Blowed if I know. I turned in fer some shut-eye long afore midnight. I'll go an' ask Rudge.'

'Make it nice and quiet. We ain't ready to spring ourselves on folk yet,' said Mal. 'Can we stable our broncs here?'

Sangster nodded. 'Help yourselves to cawfee,' he growled as he left the kitchen.

The two men saw to the dun gelding and pinto by which time Mex had returned. The three of them entered the kitchen and helped themselves to coffee. Sangster had returned with Levi Rudge who was a tall, slim, middle-aged man looking more like a scout than saloon keeper. He nodded affably to the three men.

'Howdy, Barrett. Ain't seen you fellers before,' he remarked to Mex and Clint. 'Heard plenty about you though. Bellamy and Juarez, ain't it?'

When the pards nodded, he came straight to the point.

'Stumpy came in 'bout two in the morning. He's sleeping off a man-sized drunk, but knowing him he'll be as fresh as paint soon as you go up. Just take him a drink to get the circulation going. He told me there could be some fireworks in town purty soon. Reckon he knew I'd keep my lip buttoned.'

214

'Have you seen my sister, Levi?' asked Mal.

Rudge nodded. 'Yeah. Saw her yesterday. She's staying in that dump of Murrow's. Mitchell spread it around there's gonna be a wedding tomorrow but when I saw Stella, she didn't look like she was excited any.'

'Mitchell's got his ceremonies mixed up,' said Mex with a short laugh. The frown on Clint's face and the set of his lips indicated that Mex wasn't joking.

'Well, what are we waiting for?' asked Clint, setting down his empty mug. 'Let's go and see what Hollister's got to tell us.'

Mex and Mal drank up and they all trooped out of the kitchen on Levi Rudge's heels.

Stella Barrett woke up just after sun-up and as her immediate future crowded in upon her consciousness, she tried to sink back into the safety of sleep. The noise from the street ruined her chances and with a groan she got up. As she dressed she was filled with despair. Just one more day, then, to save Mal, she would have to marry a man she now knew to be crooked and at the head of a ruthless gang who took murder in its stride.

The clamour from the street grew louder and curiosity triumphing momentarily over despair, she crossed to the window, pulled aside the curtains, and looked out.

Down below a crowd had collected round

a horse with a still figure draped over its saddle. She saw Marshal Leverson stagger out of his office and goggle at the sight as the crowd fell away from him. He pulled himself together and took hold of a note that was pinned to the dead man's back and in that instant Stella recognised the cadaver.

'Shand!' she uttered in a hoarse voice. She pulled the window down in an endeavour to hear what was being said.

'What's it say?' a sleepy eyed puncher asked Leverson as the Marshal spelled out the words.

'Never mind,' snapped Leverson. 'You go and get hold of Steve Mitchell and Murrow.' He stuffed the note in his pocket, ignoring the muttering of the crowd that surged forward to catch a view of it.

The puncher hurried away and Leverson grabbed another. 'Take the body to the funeral parlour,' Stella heard him say. 'I'll be over to check on his effects after Mulcahy's done with him.'

The crowd dispersed, most of them to go about their business, some to follow the led horse to the funeral parlour and some to take up positions where they could watch whatever moves followed this staggering event.

Stella saw Mitchell and Murrow join Leverson after a while and when Leverson had spoken a few words, Mitchell's face lost its tan. There was a wild look about him as he pushed past the Marshal and entered the gaolhouse.

There was no pity for Shand in Stella's heart. His type of man had no place amongst decent folk but an awful fear tugged at her. The last time she had seen him alive was when Clint and Mex had ridden away from the line shack ostensibly taking the bounty hunter to be dealt with by Abe Ferris, the Sheriff. And now Shand was dead.

Could it be that Clint and Mex were cold-blooded killers, prepared to gun a man down without a chance just to further their aims? So far they had only done what was necessary to help her and Mal in apparent honesty of purpose. Were they in reality men who would stop at nothing in order to bring success to any venture they happened to tackle? If such were the case, they were no better than Mitchell and his associates.

When she thought of the love that had deepened in her for Clint, and weighed him as a cold-blooded killer against Mitchell the man she was due to marry for Mal's sake, she reflected bitterly that she was between the devil and the deep blue sea.

At last she decided there must be another answer. Shand was dead – that fact was inescapable but she would not believe that Clint or Mex had done the killing for the sake of expediency.

She washed at the basin and as she dried

herself she made her decisions. For Mal's sake she would go through with the farce of marrying Mitchell but she would be a wife in name only. If he forced himself upon her then she would kill him. She would defend herself with the same brutal lack of concern that typified Mitchell and his cronies. It seemed to her that no matter how one tried to live a civilised life, the west ultimately dragged one down to the level of the scum who degraded it.

With her mind made up Stella felt more able to face the future and when she went to the dining hall, she was surprised to find she had an appetite. She was just about through when Stumpy Hollister entered. He ignored the suspicious glances from the three Lone Star punchers who were deputed to keep an eye on Stella, and sitting beside her ordered a breakfast.

There was a wealth of pleasure in the girl's eyes. In her predicament any pleasant association from the past was welcome.

'I thought you were staying on at the line shack,' she said as she smiled at the oldster.

'Yeah, but I got around to thinking I'd like fine to be on hand to see you wed.' Stumpy spoke quite loudly and with apparent sincerity. The suspicion faded from the Lone Star men's faces and gradually they ignored the girl and Hollister.

Blowing noisily on his coffee, Stumpy

managed to whisper an instruction to the girl with enough information to make her eyes gleam with happiness.

'Go to your room and stay there. Mal's safe and the showdown's mighty close.'

One of the punchers caught the tail end of the whisper and shot a suspicious look in their direction.

'Cripes, this cawfee's hot,' grunted Hollister. 'Reckon I'd be obliged if you'd have a word with Steve 'bout me staying on the payroll, Miss Stella,' he said just loud enough to reach the puncher. 'Like a durned fool I told him last night I'd quit.'

'That's alright, Stumpy,' Stella replied. Her voice was even although her heart hammered with excitement. 'I guess Steve'll do as I say.'

The Lone Star men had heard enough of the conversation to convince them Stumpy had come in just to ensure his continuity of employment and when Stella left for her room, they sat smoking and drinking coffee, taking no notice of the one-armed man.

When the firing started up outside on Main Street they were unprepared for the change in Hollister and the unwavering Colt that covered them.

'Freeze, you lobo-eared coyotes,' snarled Stumpy and the three men stiffened in their seats. 'Place your hands on the table nice and steady and keep 'em there.' The Rafter

K man grinned. 'Ain't nothing going on out there that'll save you fellers from the hoosegow.'

One of the punchers made a dive sideways but without batting an eyelid Stumpy fired once. The puncher completed his dive with a hole in his chest. The other two blanched and sat bolt upright in their seats.

'You too, come an' sit down,' Hollister said to the cook who had looked out of his kitchen in alarm.

With his eyes averted from the dead puncher, the cook walked stiffly across the room and sat down as far away from Stumpy as possible.

CHAPTER FOURTEEN

'Let me see that note!'

Steve Mitchell almost shouted the words when the door shut behind the three men. Leverson handed it over and his moustaches waggled nervously. Murrow stood beside Mitchell and stared at it. Mex had written with a bold hand:

'Returned for burying. Carcase not fit for Rafter K buzzards.'

'Bellamy and that blamed Mexican!' yelled Mitchell. 'Thought Hollister said they'd quit.' Venom gleamed in the rancher's eyes as the temper surged in him. 'I'll kill that pair of interfering saddle tramps if it's the last thing I do.'

'You can have 'em!' ground out Leverson. 'Me – I'm getting out.'

Murrow placed a hand on the Marshal's arm. The saloon keeper was quite calm.

'Just because Shand got himself shot up, there's no reason for anybody to run out of the stake we've got here. I admit that Bellamy and Juarez have had luck but that don't make 'em stack any higher. We've got the aces. Barrett's in our hands an' a gone goose. Steve's gonna get himself hitched to Stella Barrett. When that's done those two fellers'll be out on a limb. And we can take that herd back when we want to.'

Murrow's words went a long way to calming both Mitchell and Leverson and the saloon keeper poured out drinks to keep up the good work but the situation changed suddenly in a way that had him fighting to keep control.

A rider pulled up outside the gaolhouse and Mitchell at the window glared furiously as the man tethered his mount to the hitchrail. The door opened and the puncher stood in the doorway.

'Seen Steve?' he asked of Murrow and

Leverson then his eyes swivelled round to the window. He shut the door and came in.

'Bad news, Steve,' he said simply then backed away as Mitchell tore across to him. The rancher grasped the man's shirt and dragged him close.

'What bad news?' he screeched.

'They've taken Barrett,' the man managed to say. 'There's only Drew an' me left alive. The hombres that jumped us sure mean bus...' He didn't finish what he was saying. Mitchell gave him a violent push, sending him flying. Slowly the puncher picked himself up off the floor and with a disgusted look at Mitchell, helped himself to a glass of bourbon.

'Now what?' There was more than a shade of apprehension in Leverson's voice.

'You fellers can do what you like,' said Murrow at length. 'But I aim to rustle up enough men to take back that herd. I reckon the game's finished here.'

Mitchell glared at him, his face purple, but Murrow was unmoved.

'You can count me in, Slim. That's one sure profit.' Leverson made his remark with decision and Mitchell turned on him furiously.

'I'm not finished here yet,' he yelled. 'I'll still get what I'm after and nobody's going after that herd until I say so.'

Murrow's eyes slitted as he faced Mitchell

and the rancher looked from him to the Marshal warily. The puncher grabbed his drink and backed away in an attempt to get out of the line of trouble as the air in the gaolhouse became charged with tension. Nobody noticed the big schooner draw up on the other side of the street and Levi Rudge unhitch the team and lead the animals away.

Suddenly the window was shattered as a stone crashed into the room. The three men spun round in astonishment and as one they fastened their gaze on the paper wrapped round the stone. Murrow being nearest picked it up, slipped the cord away and smoothed the paper out. He read the note and passed it to the others without a word.

'When the railroad runs through Rafter K, a Barrett will be there. Stay where you are and you get the same treatment your Vigilantes gave the Rafter K. Come out and we'll be waiting.'

Signed: Barrett, Bellamy and Juarez.

Mitchell dropped the note and ran to the window like a man demented. The prairie schooner stood without its canvas covering, loaded with barrels, providing excellent cover for the men who waited. He came back to the other two.

'Those buzzards have got plenty of cover out there,' he snarled. 'Slip out the back way,

Slim, and rustle up the boys.'

Murrow was about to refuse then thought better of it. Turning away with a tight smile, he reckoned this was just the way he wanted things. He'd ride out with Mitchell's hands and take the trail herd back. If Mitchell and Leverson got what looked like coming to them, that would leave him holding a fortune.

Without a backward glance he went through the middle doorway and continued past the cells to the back exit. Slipping the bolts he opened the door a piece then slammed it shut again as a hail of buckshot crashed into the doorpost. He cursed loud and long as he made his way back to the office.

Mitchell was at the window firing bullets blindly across the street. Leverson stood in the middle of the room, seemingly stunned by the turn of events while the cowpuncher sat calmly drinking bourbon. Murrow looked at Mitchell with contempt in his cold eyes.

'You'll need that ammunition you're wasting before you're through, Mitchell,' he said.

The Lone Star man turned to glare at him as a fusillade of shots came from the other side of the street then yelled and clapped his hand to the side of his head as a part of his ear was shot clean away. He jumped away from the window and stared in amazement at the blood that dripped on to the floor. Murrow eyed him completely unmoved. The wound had the effect of calming the rancher and he reloaded his guns with precision.

'They've got one posted at the back and he's toting a shotgun,' said Murrow quietly. 'That makes just two out front. Not bad odds. There are four of us.'

The puncher topped up his glass then reached for his gun. He aimed it in the general direction of the other three.

'You've got the odds wrong,' he announced. 'If I've gotta use my shootin' iron, it'll be for ventilatin' Mitchell. No one pushes me around an' gets away with it. Anyways, I'm keepin' outa this quarrel.'

Murrow grinned in a disarming manner and half turned away from the puncher then like lightning he spun around. His gun greased out, belched flame as it cleared leather and the puncher pitched face forward on to the table.

'When I go out from here, I want no gun in my back,' Murrow said calmly.

'You're blamed right, Slim,' remarked Leverson, coming back to life. 'If there are just two out front I reckon we'd better make a move.'

'What's the hurry?' growled Mitchell. 'Let 'em sweat out there. Wait long enough and my boys'll take a hand.'

Murrow moved towards the window and looked out cautiously. The old potman Sangster of the Frontiersman was trundling a small cask along the street but there was no sign of Barrett or Bellamy. They were obviously taking no chances and were content to remain hidden behind the schooner. Murrow recognised the small cask for a tallow container just as the old man pushed it out of view to where the Rafter K men waited. He turned away from the window with a curse.

'They're not going to sweat it out, Mitchell. They're gonna burn us out like they said.'

'They wouldn't risk setting the town alight,' growled Mitchell, dabbing at the mutilated ear with his bandanna.

Murrow didn't answer but just slipped another round into his gun to replace the one he'd pumped into the puncher's chest.

In answer to Mitchell's assertion, the remaining fragments of glass splintered as a tallow-dipped torch came hurtling through the window. Murrow cursed as he ran and stamped it out, filling the air with acrid fumes, but preventing the flames from spreading. He rounded on Mitchell with a curse.

'Wouldn't risk setting the town alight eh?' he sneered. 'By my reckoning you've been plumb wrong about Barrett and those other loco fools all along.'

'Mebbe.' Mitchell snapped the word out and he glared at Murrow with all his former brash bombast back in his eye. His shoulders were squared in the old arrogant set and the blood that still flowed down his face added to his overall frightening appearance. 'But I aim to show you that I was dead right when I said I'd kill those hombres if it's the last thing I do.' He moved towards the door. 'You ready?' he asked.

Murrow shrugged and nodded coolly. Leverson looked from one to the other, his moustaches hanging low.

'Yeah,' he breathed and took up position behind Murrow.

Mal Barrett eased his position behind the big cask and grinned at Clint.

'You reckon they'll show, Bellamy?' he asked.

'Dunno,' answered Clint laconically. 'We'll give 'em a couple of minutes then we'll throw another torch in just to show we mean business.'

'You fellers gonna jest gun 'em down as they come out?' Old Sangster asked before biting off a sizeable piece of plug tobacco.

The two youngsters exchanged a quick glance then shook their heads.

'Nope. We'll give 'em an even break,' replied Clint. 'I guess we're maybe plain loco but that's the way it's gotta be if Bar-

227

rett's gonna stay around these parts.'

There was a gleam in the old man's eyes as he savoured the possibility of a bona fide gun duel.

'Reckon you'd best tell 'em then,' he added. 'An even chance should bring 'em out fast enough.' He spat a stream of tobacco juice on to the sidewalk before continuing. 'Mind, that Murrow is plain lightning with his shooting irons an' Leverson's no slouch, but Mitchell, I jest don't know. Anyways he must be mighty good to head the outfit. If it was me, I'd gun 'em down.'

'That wouldn't add up to the tales I've heard about you,' replied Mal. 'So quit talking.'

Further up the street a rapidly growing crowd of people watched and waited for something to happen. A number of Lone Star men were amongst the crowd but they were too eager to witness a gun duel to precipitate things. They reckoned Mitchell, Murrow and Leverson would weather through alright. Clint saw Stella's white face in the front of the crowd but he made no sign.

'Hey, Mitchell!' yelled out Mal. 'You coming out? If you three come out now, we'll give you an even break. Holster your guns and we'll draw for it.'

A ripple of approval came from the crowd but Stella's voice broke in sharply.

228

'No – no! Don't take any more chances!'

Clint could see her horrified expression and deep down he knew her concern was as much for him as Mal. Something else niggled at him though. 'Wonder what's happened to Hollister?' he muttered.

'I'll take a looksee,' said old Sangster even as Mitchell shouted his reply.

'We'll take you up on that, Barrett,' came the reply from inside the gaolhouse. 'When we come out, you show yourselves and draw on the count of three.' As Mitchell spoke, so old Sangster slipped across to the hotel.

Slowly the gaolhouse door opened and Mitchell led the way out on to the verandah. He was completely master of himself and ignored the blood that spilled down his face. Murrow followed, inscrutable, cold and deadly. Leverson came more slowly. The set of his moustaches showed his heart wasn't in it. Their guns were holstered.

Mal and Clint exchanged glances. They were calm and unafraid but with both of them the saliva had dried up, their nerve ends tingled and their hearts pumped just that much faster.

'I guess Mitchell's yours, Mal,' said Clint quietly. 'I'll take Murrow first then go for Leverson if I'm still around.'

Mal forced a grin to his face showing a confidence that did Clint a power of good to see. 'Best of luck, Bellamy,' he said.

Clint smiled back then they stepped out one either end of Levi Rudge's schooner.

The mutterings of the crowd stopped at once and the morning air became charged with tension as the men faced each other. Now that the chips were down Leverson looked every bit as menacing as the men who flanked him. He and Mitchell stood with hands hanging low near their six-guns while Murrow, eyes slitted, seemingly detached from the whole proceedings, had his hands out of sight behind his back.

To the onlookers it was apparent that the odds of three to two had filled the three men with confidence and the crowd took stock of Barrett and Bellamy again, seeking out signs of fear. They saw none. Both Barrett, straddle-legged, lithe and eager, and Bellamy, grim and wide-shouldered, were keyed for action.

Mitchell took a look up the street.

'Hey, Grogan,' he yelled. 'Count up to three and make it loud.'

The puncher Grogan stepped out a bit in front of the crowd. There was a pause then his voice pierced the still air clearly.

'One!'

It was only a second before the man called again but it seemed to stretch into eternity. Clint fastened his gaze on Murrow's face in the hope of detecting a sign of indecision but the suspicion of a smile on the saloon keeper's face only served to sharpen his senses to possible trickery.

'Two!' Grogan intoned and no one noticed the rapid hoofbeats as a rider rode into town from the south.

The intake of breath taken by the protagonists and onlookers was audible above the hoofbeats as time hung then Grogan yelled:

'Three!'

In the split second that Clint clawed for his guns he saw the blue muzzle of the Derringer in Murrow's hand and he knew the reason for the smile. He threw himself sideways and down, bringing his guns into play as he hit the dust with a thud. He sensed Mal Barrett fall from Murrow's first shot and felt the tug of the bullet that plucked his Stetson from off his head; then his guns wrought havoc.

Murrow stiffened and clutched his abdomen a fraction before Leverson slumped over into him. They rolled to the ground together. Mitchell, already wounded from Mal's first lightning shot, held himself upright by sheer willpower and with his face twisted through hate and pain, emptied his gun in Clint's general direction.

The Texan held his fire as he saw Mitchell's gun droop and the bullets fall short of their mark. He came to his feet as the Lone Star boss slumped back against the timber front of the gaolhouse and slid to the sidewalk. The rider, Abe Ferris, reined his horse in and surveyed the scene.

As Clint crossed to Barrett's side, so Stella came running. There was deep anxiety in her lovely blue eyes as she stooped down over her brother but she clasped Clint's arm in a grip that told him exactly how she felt.

Mal was smiling when they turned him over.

'I'm alright,' he said quietly. 'I reckon I got Mitchell before that coyote Murrow did his sleight of hand.'

Tears of relief flooded Stella's eyes as Mal spoke. Clint leaned over and gave her shoulder a pat before giving his attention to the crowd who were now surging forward to view the result of the battle.

Grogan and the other Lone Star punchers had eased themselves back out of the crowd and Clint, after a glance across to Abe Ferris tethering his horse outside the gaolhouse, pushed his way through the excited citizens and followed the Lone Star men into the hotel. As he stood in the foyer, Mex and Levi Rudge joined him.

'Nice work, Clint,' said Mex, his white teeth gleaming in a wide smile. 'How's Barrett?'

'He'll do. Murrow was palming a Derringer and put a bullet through him just under the shoulder blade.' Clint pointed up the stairs. 'I reckon Mitchell's men have gone up to collect their warbags. You stay here and cover the stairs with that shotgun. Levi and me and Mex'll take a look around.'

Rudge nodded and the pards toured the downstairs rooms. When they came to the kitchen, old Sangster was framed in the doorway, the six-guns in his hands seeming too heavy for his meagre frame to bear. He grinned a toothless greeting.

'We've got a couple of the bastards in here, fellers, an' one that's gonna leave feet first.'

He stood aside for Clint and Mex to enter. Stumpy Hollister was sitting easily, his gun covering the two Lone Star punchers and the cook unwaveringly.

'Glad to see you fellers all in one piece,' he remarked. 'I was getting mighty tired of covering these coyotes. I guess a few more minutes and I'd have salivated 'em just to end the chore.'

'Don't know what's eaten into the crazy galoot,' snarled one of the punchers. 'He just jumped us when we was finishing our cawfee and gunned down Ed Newsome.'

There was no sympathy on the faces of the pards. Clint nodded curtly to the door.

'Get moving,' he grated. 'We'll let Abe Ferris sort you fellers out.'

The Lone Star men got out of their seats grudgingly and walked in front of the pards to the entrance hall where another half-dozen men stood on the stairs eyeing Levi

Rudge warily. Rudge had a reputation for handling a shotgun to create the maximum damage, and with Mitchell, Murrow and Leverson either dead or in custody, the Lone Star hands saw no profit in risking physical injury at Levi's hands. They came downstairs obediently enough when ordered by Mex and with Rudge preceding them, filed quietly out into the street.

The crowd outside the gaolhouse fell away as the huddle of Lone Star men were herded along under the guns of their captors. Abe Ferris stood up from the still body of Leverson and followed them through the door.

'I reckon you'd better take these hombres over, Ferris,' said Clint. 'They're all Mitchell's men and I'm blamed sure they're tied up in all of Mitchell's schemes.'

Ferris unhitched the keys from a nail on the wall and led the way to the cells. With the Lone Star men safely under lock and key he returned to the office followed by the two pards, Rudge, Hollister and Sangster.

'You fellers didn't leave much for me to do,' he growled. 'But from what Leverson told me before he cashed in his cheques, you sure did right to go ahead. Anyways he squared Barrett for that killing of Faro. He saw Faro go for his gun afore Barrett. He said Murrow wrote out all those bills of sale forging the signatures and Luke Mappin just added his own signature and the date.

Murrow had collected the specimen signatures from Fargo staging depots along the route.' Ferris paused and lit a cigarette. 'It seems the whole gang were together down on the Neuces a long time ago and met up again at Kansas City before moving in on Dallin. I reckon they were doing alright until you fellers showed up.'

Clint wasn't interested in praise at that moment. Now that things were squared up he wanted to be at Stella Barrett's side. He crossed to the doorway and looked out over the crowd but there was no sign of Stella or the wounded man.

'Barrett's being fixed by the sawbones,' Ferris said, reading Clint's thoughts. 'His sister's along with him.'

The Texan pushed out through the crowd, ignoring the plaudits of men who had been eager enough before to toady up to Mitchell and his crew. He crossed the street to the doctor's house with Mex just a few paces behind. In his eagerness he pushed the door open and entered uninvited. Mex came in more slowly.

Stella was standing beside the couch watching the doctor swab Mal's wound but when Clint burst in she rushed towards him and unashamedly threw her arms around his neck. She hugged him the more as the tension drained out of her until at last Clint held her from him and looked deep into her eyes now misty with tears of happiness. He kissed her simply, without passion, but more in the manner of sealing a bargain. Then with his arm around her he walked to the couch where Mal Barrett was watching them with a glint of humour in his eyes.

'Y'know, Bellamy,' he said. 'I just couldn't understand why you and your pard stuck your necks out so far on my account. Seems I wasn't thinking straight from the word go.'

Clint grinned and Stella blushed. 'Knowing you like I do now, Mal, I guess I'd side you for your own sake,' Clint replied. 'And that goes for Mex too, I reckon.'

Mex who had stood by watching the display of affection with an amused expression eased up to Clint and whispered in his ear. The Texan turned Stella round to face him and for a moment he was serious.

'Mex has to be moving on, Stella, and he just hates to miss a wedding. He reckons you and me should keep that date with the minister. I'd be mighty pleased if you agree with him.'

The girl nodded happily and turned to Mex with a bright smile.

'You get the nicest ideas, Mex,' she said then turning back to Clint impulsively: 'If there's to be a wedding tomorrow then there are things for me to do today. You two can come to see me and Mal at the Frontiersman tonight.'

236

Gently but firmly she propelled them out on to the sidewalk. The two pardners leaned on the verandah rail and looked at Dallin with new interest now that the fear of sudden death had been removed.

As Clint lit up a cigarette and Mex dug in his pocket for a cheroot, the drover Rimmer rode past on his way out of town. He gave them a sour look then turned his gaze to the south. It was only when he passed the grim cortège taking the bodies of Mitchell and the men who had died with him to the funeral parlour that his expression changed. It struck him he was darned lucky to be riding out with a whole skin. He cast a look behind to where Clint and Mex smoked contentedly.

'Blamed if it don't pay to be honest,' he thought.

The publishers hope that this book has given you enjoyable reading. Large Print Books are especially designed to be as easy to see and hold as possible. If you wish a complete list of our books please ask at your local library or write directly to:

The Golden West Large Print Books
Magna House, Long Preston,
Skipton, North Yorkshire.
BD23 4ND

This Large Print Book, for people
who cannot read normal print,
is published under the auspices of

THE ULVERSCROFT FOUNDATION